Story of
ACHU

Andrew Pappachen

STORY OF ACHU
Copyright © 2020 by Andrew Pappachen

All rights reserved. No part of this publication may be reproduced, distributed, or transmitted in any form or by any means, including photocopying, recording, or other electronic or mechanical methods, without the prior written permission of the publisher or author, except in the case of brief quotations embodied in critical reviews and certain other noncommercial uses permitted by copyright law.

Although every precaution has been taken to verify the accuracy of the information contained herein, the author and publisher assume no responsibility for any errors or omissions. No liability is assumed for damages that may result from the use of information contained within.

Library of Congress Control Number: 2020920780
ISBN-13: Paperback: 978-1-64749-258-8
ePub: 978-1-64749-259-5

Printed in the United States of America

GoToPublish LLC
1-888-337-1724
www. Gotopublish. Com
info@gotopublish. Com

CONTENTS

Introduction v
Chapter 1 1
Chapter 2 13
Chapter 3 25
Chapter 4 37
Chapter 5 47
Chapter 6 57
Chapter 7 67
Chapter 8 79
Chapter 9 91
Chapter 10 101
Chapter 11 111
Chapter 12 125
Chapter 13 135
Chapter 14 145

INTRODUCTION

Along with narrating the story of Achu, a fictional character, born in Kerala, India 80 years ago in a poor farm worker family and died in USA after having a successful career in investment banking. As the story is narrated discussion is diverted to the historic events and circumstances, life in poverty, kingdoms and feudalism in India before becoming a democratic republic after the British rule, various forms of political ideologies like socialism, communism and capitalism, investment banking and wealth accumulation, life's event involving death, birth, good times and bad times, a changing family structure, luxury life in USA, presidential elections and economic impacts and finally the impact of pandemic. The author depicts a fictional story to provide some of the facts of life and how a person born in poverty can become a rich person in capitalistic America through education and hard work while facing the various events and mishaps in building a family. The author expects readers to learn how a person through hard work, determination, and education can help reach the goals of life. The author also wants the readers to know that life flows through various opportunities, experiences and realities and most of the events are unpredictable. After facing all the events throughout the life, end of life comes so fast and unexpected. Author expects the readers to enjoy reading the book while riding through various experiences of Achu's condition. Humans think and act similarly everywhere struggling through day to day events and activities to survive. Getting wealthy is everybody's ambition, but very few people in the World become wealthy. Wealthy does not mean happy.

Achu Narayanan is a fictional character born in 1940 in a very poor farm worker family in Kerala, India. He takes advantage of the educational opportunities in that State, ultimately migrates to USA for higher studies and become a wealthy investment banker. The story is written with the background of contemporary political, cultural and economic situations so that readers can travel through the time.

Pictures of Kerala, India in 1940s

A hut

Two women crushing rice

Farm - bullock used to move triller

A kerosene lamp

CHAPTER 1

In a remote area, southwest corner of India, there was a beautiful village surrounded by shallow backwaters. It was a small island with streams and rivers. There were coconut trees everywhere. One could hear the birds chirping, frogs croaking, and dogs barking. About 250 families lived there.

Small villages nearby were also surrounded by water. The shallow waters around these villages become paddy fields during dry season. Cultivation is done only once a year when the water levels are very low. On land, the main cultivation is coconut. Most of the villagers are farmworkers. The owners of the farms are mostly rich and are called landlords.

In 1940, Achu was born in one of the villages to a poor young farmworker couple. Later on, his two younger sisters were also born. His family, along with his grandparents, lived in a small hut made of mud and thatched roof, with two rooms and a cooking area. Their home was built in the land owned by one of the rich farmers.

Seven people somehow managed to live in the small hut. The only income for Achu's family was the daily wage his parents earn working in the farm. They had a seasonal job, and other times, they barely worked.

During the farming and cultivation time, they could manage a fairly good life; but during the wet season, they did not have enough income to feed the family. If there was no work, they barely ate; oftentimes, they starved.

Living in poverty—often not having enough food to eat, not having enough space to sleep, and not having enough clothes to wear—was the destiny of Achu and his family.

In terms of clothing, Achu's grandparents hardly cover their body. They used wraps that covers the bottom part of the body, also known as a *mundu*. His grandmother wore another piece of cloth to cover her chest. His mother paired her *mundu* with a blouse.

Almost everybody in those villages had similar way of life. Most of the time, their meal was boiled rice soup. Sometimes, they get a jackfruit or some yucca from the landlords.

Because the area was surrounded by water, fish was part of the meal often. They fish using a small net or a fishing rod. Coconut, which was also common in the island, they sometimes eat coconut and drink coconut water. Nothing was in abundance, but Achu's family managed like most of the people around the neighborhood.

Their situation was similar to the ones who lived in Medieval Europe. These feudal leaders or landowners are the ones who paid the taxes to the kings and emperors, and therefore, they got the favors from the kings.

In the year that Achu was born, the Kingdom of Travancore ruled. The poor people were not taken care of. They were suffering. Some belong in the working class or the *shudra*, and there were also some in the lowest level of the caste system, the untouchables or *dalit*. They had no rights because they do not pay taxes; they are not even allowed to enter the landlord's house except for cleaning or other related work. They always stand outside when they go to talk to the landlord.

The caste system in India discriminated the untouchables and were not given any opportunity to grow economically or get education. Achu's grandparents never went to school. His father only went to primary school, and his mother never did

Second World War began in late 1939, months before Achu was born. World War did not have much impact in Achu's neighborhood, even though many from there joined the British army and died in the war.

The war was the result of overzealous and the supremacy ideals of the German dictator Adolf Hitler, the fascist ideals of Italy's prime minister Benito Mussolini, and the ambition of Japanese Emperor Hirohito to expand his power to Asia and Pacific. They formed the Axis, which was challenged by the Allies headed by Great Britain, USA, and the Soviet Union and was joined by some European countries and China.

World War II ended in 1945 with the Allies defeating the Axis. The Indian Army fought with the Allied forces as part of British Army. However, the Indian National Congress, which was led by Mahatma Gandhi, was fighting for independent India at that time and refused to support the war and started the Quit India Movement in August 1942.

British rulers of India jailed most of the congress leaders until the end of war. During this time, one of the congress leaders, Subhas Chandra Bose, split with the party and formed the Indian National Army (INA) with the help of Japanese forces. The army consisted of Indian prisoners of war who were captured in Singapore. They joined with Japan to fight against the British army and the Allies and, ultimately, to liberate India from British rule. However, INA was badly defeated, and Subhas Chandra Bose died of a plane accident near Taiwan while escaping from Singapore to Japan.

About 87,000 Indian soldiers (India included current Pakistan, Bangladesh, and Nepal) died in this war. Indian army was a major support to the British army, who fought with the Allied forces and finally defeated the Axis. About 70 to 85 million people died in the war, mostly civilians in Soviet Union and China.

The biggest atrocity of the Second World War was the Holocaust—genocide of six million European Jews by the Hitler and the Nazis through mass shootings and extermination in concentration camps and gas chambers. Adolf Hitler was the leader of the Nazi Party and was Chancellor of Germany from 1933 to 1945. He killed himself by gunshot on April 30, 1945, after surrendering to the Allies.

Benito Mussolini, the Italian fascist dictator, was executed on April 28, 1944, by an Italian partisan in a village in Northern Italy.

Japan continued the war until America dropped the first atomic bomb over the City of Hiroshima on August 6, 1945, and on Nagasaki on August 9, 1945. After the huge destruction of life by the atomic bombs, US President Harry Truman asked the Japanese emperor to surrender. On August 15, 1945, Emperor Hirohito of Japan surrendered to the Allies. Hirohito, the 124th emperor of Japan, continued to be the emperor until 1947, when Japan achieved democracy.

Second World War resulted in great economic destruction all over the world. But for Achu and his family, the war had no impact. They did not know much about the war or the involvement of Indian and British army. They were so poor and isolated from access to regular information from newspapers or radio.

This was the situation with all the poor people in India and across the world. Poor people remained poor. The countries involved in the war lost many of their citizens, industries, and wealth. It was a very difficult time for Achu and his family, with no real source for any help.

Achu and his siblings used to sleep in one room with the grandparents on the mud floor with mats made of palm leaves. They had no pillows, and three people covered their bodies with a cotton sheet. His parents slept in the other room.

Before going to sleep, their grandmother used to tell them stories about the devil and Yakshi. According to her story, a yakshi (female ghost of a woman who died unhappily) used to live in the next island. A yakshi appears as a young lady to people who walk in the dark, and when they go near her, she turns into a cruel creature and kills them.

The story about the devil was different. According to her, the devil is ugly and tall and walks with long chains on the shoulder at night in the neighborhood. If someone walks alone at night, the devil will kill and eat him.

Because of these scary stories, they were afraid to go out at night. But for these three children, sleeping together with grandparents was the most enjoyable time in their childhood. They could not enjoy playing that much. During the day, children in the neighborhood played outside. They had no toys to play with, so they made their own ball with coconut leaves. Although they did not have much, they enjoyed the outdoors and playing with makeshift toys.

The school year starts in the middle of June. At the age of five, Achu was put in a government primary school, which was two miles away from his house when traveled by foot. Since there was no kindergarten class, he was put in the first grade.

His official name was Achu Narayanan; his father's name being the last name.

The neighborhood children of the poor farmworkers walked together to school every day, about 30 minutes each way. The children of the farm owners, since they have the luxury to spend for education, ride daily to school; some were in boarding school.

Government schools had limited facilities, and since all the students were from poor families, the overall education of the children never reached the level of private schools.

Achu liked the school; he made lot of friends. Walking with his friends to school was fun, even though most of them did not have sufficient food to eat and had just one set of clothes, which needed to be washed and dried on Sundays. If it rains on Sundays, the clothes do not get washed, so sometimes they smelled bad. They had limited resources to clean themselves. To clean their teeth, they used their fingers dipped in salt and burned rice skins.

That was the life Achu and his friends experienced during their childhood life: starving occasionally, not having enough clothes to wear, and walking two miles to and from school every day.

Aside from living in a small space in their small thatched mud house, they also had no bathrooms or toilets, so they just used any available spot they can hide or river banks if they need to do necessary daily routines.

That part in India has a forty-day rainy season that happens between June and July, although rain is a regular thing even normal season. During monsoon, the area gets flooded, sometimes entering their hut.

The school buildings were poorly maintained. The roofs leaked during the rain. Some schools closed for few days because of heavy rains. Some rains could be tolerable, so classes continued. When the school remained open, the children walked in the flood.

This was normal to Achu. That was the lifestyle of the poor children in the neighborhood, and he was no different. However, this community of the poor lived happily together.

In his free time, Achu often went to the river shore. He liked to look far into the horizon and think about his future. He saw how the rich landlords and their families lived with abundance while his family struggled to make a living every day.

It did give him a little bit of comfort when his grandfather told him that their life now was better. When his grandfather was a child, they used to live in small shacks, which was worse.

The villages surrounded by water were divided by streams and rivers. Bridges made from coconut trees tied together were built. They raised from six to ten feet so that big wooden row boats could go under.

Land transportation was not available since there were no roads through those villages. People walked for miles to reach their destinations or nearby town. For farther destinations or for transporting goods, they took a boat.

There were small islands everywhere with coconut trees. It was beautiful, serene, with clear skies and fresh air.

Achu and everybody in the family took baths in these rivers and streams daily. They had to go on the boat to collect well water from a dry land far away.

Life was difficult and hard, but they never felt it like that, everything was normal to them, including the poverty and starvation. They experienced this for generations. Many of the older people have never seen cars, buses, or trains during their life. Farmers used to keep small chicken and cattle farms to provide eggs and milk. For poor people, eggs and milk were dream food. This type of poverty was all over India in villages and rural areas. These people strived to make a living.

The area where Achu and family lived was ruled by the King of Travancore, one of the more than five hundred autonomous kingdoms in India. Travancore royal family was ruling this kingdom in the southwestern end of India for more than 150 years. The last Maharaja was Sree Chithira Thirunal Bala Ramavarma, who ruled till 1949 when the kingdom merged in the newly formed free India. These kings lived in luxury taxing rich people and collecting revenue from most of the farmlands owned by the kingdom.

As the Second World War ended in 1945, all congress leaders were released from jail. After the war, the freedom movement became stronger, and demonstrations were accelerated under the leadership of the Indian National Congress led by Mahatma Gandhi.

When the British agreed to give independence, the leader of the All-India Muslim League, Muhammad Ali Jinnah, asked for a separate country for Muslims. Therefore, when British announced independence, they divided India and Pakistan (East and West Pakistan). East Pakistan later became an independent country named Bangladesh. Constituent assembly was already set up in early 1946, and the province elections were already conducted. Congress got 69 percent of the vote.

On Sept 2, 1946, a government was formed with Jawaharlal Nehru as the prime minister taking charge of independent India on August 15, 1947. British Viceroy Lord Mountbatten continued as the governor general until Dec. 15, 1950, when Chakravarti Rajagopalachari, an Indian, swore in.

When India became independent, Achu was in third grade. He remembered big Independence Day celebrations everywhere, even in his school. People of India were happy; they now live in an Independent country, free from the British rule.

A new state was formed with two kingdoms combining Travancore and Cochin, which also had a new government with Pattom Thanu Pillai as chief minister. People found new hope, especially the poor.

The new constitution was adopted in 1949, and on January 26, 1951, India became a democratic republic. Prime Minister Jawaharlal Nehru introduced the first five-year plan, which was the model for centralized economic planning and development. Aside from economic development through industrialization and agricultural development, village-based development plans were also implemented.

For Achu, his family, and the poor villagers, there was no major change in their lives. They were still totally dependent on the landlords. The feudalistic system continued in India even after independence. There were some small-time farmers also, who worked in their farms along with other workers. These people worked hard in their farms. Meanwhile the big landowners lived in abundance.

The Communist Party of India, which was formed in 1925, continued to challenge the congress party. It became the party of the workers and the poor. They took a stand against the landlords, who took advantage of the working poor and fought for increased salaries and benefits. India was going through the transition.

There were great divisions in the society aside from rich and poor, there were the higher caste, working caste, and the lower caste. There was also caste according to family skills, like carpenters, blacksmith, goldsmith, masons, barbers, and they were considered lower caste. Achu knew only a little about the caste system, but he certainly knew that because they were poor, they were treated badly by landowners.

Achu was now eleven years old and in middle school. His sisters were still in primary school. To go to the new school, he had to walk more than four miles, about an hour from his house.

Achu was very interested in school. Many of his schoolmates in the village dropped out after primary school. Since his parents and grandparents never got the opportunity to attend school, they encouraged him to study.

The school was owned by government. The new democratic government started changing the school curriculum.

In middle school, they had to learn Math, Malayalam, English, Indian history, Basic science, Social studies, and new Civic rules. Achu was the top student in the class for all subjects. He never joined athletics or sports because after school, he had to walk one hour to get home and he still had to make time to do his homework. Once reaching home, he did not play with his sisters or his friends in the neighborhood. He always read and studied.

There was no electricity in his village or most of the villages in India. The kerosene lamps do not provide much light. Therefore, Achu made it sure to complete his studies before sunset or study after sunrise.

This was again the normal routine for Achu. Everything was the same until something tragic happened. Achu's grandfather died after getting sick with fever. This affected the family, most especially Achu who was close to his grandparents. He died without having to experience a good life. Their grandmother was never left alone after her husband's death. Achu and his siblings continued to sleep beside her at night and listen to her stories.

Despite the difficulties in life, Achu completed middle school. At that time, he already understood that his parents, grandparents, and generations before them lived in poverty, and as farmworkers, they were totally dependent on the landlords to survive.

When India became a democratic republic, Prime Minister Jawaharlal Nehru introduced his five-year plans and declared to give importance to education and industrialization as tools for economic development. But Achu's family and all their neighbors along with more than 50 percent of the people in India remained poor, and they did not find a way out of their poverty.

In high school Achu remained top in the class. Teachers were very proud of him. In the government schools, it was unusual to find an extremely smart student in the class because when they go back home, they are faced with poverty and starvation. Achu was different. His priority was to get high grades in the class. He did not want to end up like his parents and grandparents. He wanted to have a degree, get a good job and lift his family from poverty. He knew that education is the only way he can get out of poverty.

CHAPTER 2

The year before Achu completed high school, something big happened. The States Reorganisation Act 1956 merged the district of Malabar, some parts of Travancore-Cochin (excluding four southern taluks, and the taluk of Kasargod, South Kanara. These merged areas are now known as Kerala. This government initiative was done by combining areas that speak the same language. This again brought hope to the poor, especially to Achu who was prioritizing education among others.

Achu passed with flying colors and was awarded an SSLC Secondary School Leaving Certificate, a certificate given to those who finished the program. He was so excited when he got it in the mail. He was second rank in the whole state, which rarely happened there. It was great news and an honor to the country. Journalists came to their house to interview him. At that time there was no TV broadcasting in India. Even radio was rare. The whole village gathered in front of the house, and there was a big celebration.

He wanted to enter college, but Achu's parents had no money to send him there. Achu felt hopeless until he found out from his school headmaster that scholarships were available for top rank students.

He got admission to Kerala University College in the Capital City Trivandrum. He enrolled for a three-year degree program that started after the one-year pre-university course.

Although Achu's parents had no money to purchase clothes and pay for travel to Trivandrum, he was still able to go. Luckily, he was able to borrow money from the landlord, Thomas Varghese. Everyone was showing their support for Achu, since he was the first in the village to go to college. His family and the whole village were there to send him off.

Achu was going away from his home first time in his life. He took the bus from nearby town and reached Trivandrum, which was a whole new world for him. He had never been away from home or to a town. He looked around with excitement and walked from the bus station with his bag towards the Kerala University College after asking direction from the bus driver.

He was not familiar with anything and somehow managed to reach the main office. Once there, he introduced himself and showed the certificate. They helped him fill up the necessary forms for scholarship, admission, and dormitory entrance. He shared the room with another student. All his life he was sleeping on a mat on the mud floor sharing a sheet with his sisters. Here he was in a big building in a furnished room with bed, sheet, pillows, and a study table. There was toilet and shower on every floor. In their village, Achu used to study sitting under a tree and the branches extended above the water were his toilet. He could not believe what he was seeing in the dormitory and did not even know how to use these facilities.

He never had full meals, never had the experience of formally serving on a dining table, and never experienced such luxuries. Here, he had to go to the dining room and was served good nutritious food on the table. There was sink to wash his hands and mouth.

These were all strange things for a person who grew up in poverty in a little hut in a poor village with not enough facilities to use. Life was turned upside down for Achu.

There were no phones or cell phones at that time. He wrote all about his new college and dormitory facilities to his family.

His roommate was from another part of Kerala from a family of farmers and also was a scholarship holder. His name was John and was 4th in rank in the state. They became friends and shared stories about where they came from and their families. John's parents were farmers who lived in the hilly areas of Kerala and came from different backgrounds and circumstances.

Classes started, and Achu witnessed different types of classrooms. This time English was taught as the first language in classes, and they could choose to learn either Malayalam or Hindi as their second language. Achu chose Malayalam for he was fascinated with its literature.

It took several weeks for Achu to familiarize the school, the dormitory, his classmates, and the city. He made lot of friends, but his main focus was his studies. He often used to sit alone and think about his family and what type of life they were having. He used to walk around the city and see the palace where the old King of Travancore lived and the beautiful roads and other luxurious palaces around. He used to go in front of the famous Padmanabhaswamy temple. He thought of how the King lived in such a luxury, by taxing the landlords and businesspeople, while the poor families had nothing.

The first break from college was for Onam, a great celebration of the coming of Emperor Maveli. Achu was excited to go home. He managed to save some money from the scholarship payments, so he bought clothes for his family.

Everybody was excited to see him. Achu looked different. He gained weight, dressed better, and looked like an adult. The first night he was there, he was getting ready to sleep on the floor with his sisters and grandmother, who told them the story of Marthanda Varma, the king of Travancore, who ruled and conquered other small kings around him.

Achu told his sisters that he had seen the palace of the king, and they were very curious and asked him to take them there. He promised that he will take them to Trivandrum during summer vacation.

In the morning when Achu woke up, he walked toward the river and looked at the rising sun. He had seen it many times, but this time the rising sun gave him new hopes. He promised to himself to study hard, get a good job, help his family. He dreamed for his sisters to get a good education and to build a good and comfortable house for his parents. He looked at the horizon and thought about the new world he was living in, which he wanted to explore.

Onam is a big celebration in Kerala, India. Emperor Maveli, who ruled Kerala many years ago, brought happiness and abundance to people during his time. According to the legend, Emperor Maveli, also known as Mahabali, became so popular and powerful that he was able to extend his kingdom to heavens. At that time, according to the Hindu epic, Indra pleaded to Mahavishnu (the God), to stop Mahabali from expanding his power. Vishnu transformed into a dwarf named Vamana and went to Earth. Mahabali was doing his yearly Yajna and giving people their wishes. Vamana appeared in front of Mahabali and asked for his wishes.

At that time, Mahabali was warned that Vamana is Vishnu and the God came to destroy him. Mahabali said that he already offered him and that he could not take back his word. Vamana asked for three footsteps of land, which is actually a small land. As soon as Mahabali granted the wish, Vamana transformed into Mahavishnu and measured the first step, which covered the heaven; second step covered the lower world; and Mahabali knew that when he would take the third step, it will cover the Earth and destroy it. Mahabali requested Vishnu to step on his head. Vishnu's third step pushed Mahabali to the lower world and while he was doing it gave Mahabali a wish to visit his people once a year.

That homecoming day of Mahabali is Onam; also it is the Harvest Festival. Everybody has a lavish vegetarian meal with twenty-six delicious dishes with rice. After the meal all neighborhood came out, sang, and played together.

Poor people were given free rice and vegetables for Onam. The landlords also gave rice and money to all their dependent farmworkers. The festival lasts for 10 days. Achu went back to college after the event. He told his family that he would be back during the next break, which was Christmas and New Year.

Achu continued to focus on his studies. His roommate John accompanied him most of the time. One day, John asked him more about his family and their lifestyle. Achu told him that they belonged to the lower caste and he could afford college only because of the scholarship. John told him that they were also not rich and that the scholarship helped him get the admission and meet the expenses. They decided to study together and work hard without hanging out too much with other students. John was more into science, while Achu liked economics better.

Achu went home during Christmas–New Year break and spent time with the family. He saved some money and gave it to his father.

He was very worried about the life of his family with no help in sight. Achu was determined that one day when he completes his degree program and gets a job, he could help his family. Meanwhile both his sisters were in high school.

After New Year, both Achu and John came back to the college. The final exam was in March, and they concentrated on their studies further. After the final exam, they both went back home wishing good luck and promising to meet during the summer vacation.

Achu decided to find a job so that he can make money for his future studies. He asked the landlord whether he can give him a job. The landlord gave him a job to help in his coir factory. Coir is made from the inside fiber of coconut husk and therefore the raw material was plenty there. Coir manufacturing dates back to several centuries and was mostly done by hand.

The first coir factory was established by an Irishman, James Darrah, in the mid-nineteenth century at Alapuzha, Kerala. It is an ecofriendly industry. Achu worked in the factory for two months and made the landlord happy. He also earned enough while working.

Meanwhile the results of his pre-university exam were published in the newspapers, and several journalists came looking for him again. Achu got the first rank. All newspapers covered his picture and the story of his family. Crowds gathered around his house. Achu was astonished. His family were proud and very happy. His landlord and family came with gift and money. People from nearby villages came to see him. Achu was humbled. He thanked everybody. Even though many people suggested that he should go for medicine or engineering, Achu decided to continue his degree in economics for which he would definitely get scholarship in Kerala University.

Achu joined the classes at Kerala University on June 1957. It was a three-year program, which he should complete by 1960. There was no semester system in India at that time. There was one final exam at the end of three years for major and minor subjects.

John and Achu were in different dormitories. They promised to see each other during summer time, but Achu couldn't because he had a job. His new roommate was also studying economics, and they spent time discussing and sharing class materials and studying together.

A major bill was passed by the communist government of the State of Kerala. They passed a land reform bill in 1957 and agrarian relations bill in 1958. As a result, the feudal landlords were put limitations on how much land they could hold unless registered as an estate, and each landlord was required to give free land to all farmworkers living in their land, like Achu's parents, and provide them support to build their own house in their own land.

These new reforms changed the society in Kerala and gave new rights to the poor farmworkers. Achu's parents along with few other dependent families were given land in the same area, and they all built new houses. In fact a new housing colony was created. This was a revolutionary idea to bring equality among the landowners and the poor working class.

Achu's family was very happy and they found new meaning to life. These new developments were topic of discussion in Achu's economic class. In fact, the University organized a debate to discuss this issue. Achu was the team leader of the group which supported the new reforms. Being the family member benefiting from the reform, it was easy for Achu to debate the issue strongly. He argued that the land reforms helped end the feudalistic society of the dependent farmworkers on the landlords permanently for generations with no opportunity for economic growth. They also helped transform permanently the agrarian sector, legitimize the right of the peasants, and to avoid exploitations and inequalities. A good majority of the audience agreed with the arguments of Achu and the group.

During the first two years, there were common classes for English and Malayalam, where students who have taken different majors came together. They were large classes of sixty to eighty students. It was interesting to learn both English and Malayalam literature.

Achu found special attraction to William Shakespeare's tragic dramas, *King Lear* and *Macbeth*. In fact, he joined the Shakespeare Club in the university and acted in their school play of *Macbeth*. He also liked Malayalam poetry written by great poets, like Kumaranasan and Vallathol. He joined the Malayalam Poetry Club and used to read their works in gatherings.

Achu was not interested in sports. He was more into reading, discussion, and debates. He spent his spare time in the library. During Onam and Christmas breaks he used to go home.

During the summer after the first year his grandmother passed away. He was very sad. He remembered those ghost stories Grandma used to tell them before going to sleep and her expression of great love even in the middle of extreme poverty. Conditions of Achu's family was better now. They have a little house and small property to cultivate. One of Achu's sisters will graduate SSLC the following year.

Achu had an opportunity to compare the three political systems while learning economics: the democratic socialism in India, the capitalism in western nations including USA, and the communist/socialist systems in USSR and China. The evolution of socialism in the democratic system of government in independent India came from the principles of Indian National Congress party who ruled India for many years.

Socialism is the transformation of the society to improve the condition of the working class by providing them equal opportunities and government control of all basic services. For the congress, it was a means to eliminate feudalism. Many of the large industries were nationalized, which means there was a transfer of ownership to the government. Socialism is a theory that production and distribution should be owned and managed by the state and wealth to be equally distributed.

Capitalism is an economic system that is mainly controlled by private enterprise. Corporate ownership of capital goods by private investment and process, production, and distribution of goods are determined by competition in a free market. In a communist system or a Marxist-Leninist socialism in USSR, goods are owned in common and available to all as needed and elimination of private ownership completely. It will be a totalitarian government controlled by one party rule, and all means of production and distribution are controlled by the government.

Being a victim of the feudal society, Achu liked the democratic socialism in India and opposed to the communist ideology because of lack of freedom for ordinary people. However, he was more interested to learn about capitalism, where he sees wealth is created much faster. For him, it gives opportunity for an individual to grow with hard work, sort of survival of the fittest. He knew that because Indian Democratic Socialism came out of a feudal and caste systems, the old feudal leaders and educated group, or the upper caste, still had control of the government and good jobs and his survival under these conditions would not be easy. The only way he could survive and be successful is by outsmarting people around him with government scholarships for higher education. He was determined to make use of the opportunities and become a wealthy person to bring his family and himself out of poverty.

Achu's third year started in June 1959, and at the same time, his other sister completed high school with distinction, got the scholarship, and joined the university college for pre-university course. She was in a women's dormitory. Achu now has a family member closer to him. He was very happy.

He studied various aspects of the economic development of a country and also financial investments and growths. He learned about various countries and systems around the world. He was fascinated on how USA, the world's oldest democratic country, developed so fast and he knew individual growth happened with hard work.

India was completing the second five-year plan, saw some industrial developments, but agricultural development did not reach its goal and educational systems needed much more advancement. Even though the vison of a democratic socialism is good, the politicians, government, and the systems were highly corrupt and inefficient. He was thinking about his future and how he could develop a career. At that time, becoming a bank officer was the best job for an economics degree holder or he could go for higher studies, get a master's degree, and take the Indian Administrative Service (IAS) examination and become a government official.

Achu focused on his studies during the third year of his degree program, lots of reading and research. He wanted to achieve top rank again so that he could get scholarship and go for graduate studies. He was thinking of entering Indian Institute of Management in Bangalore if he could get admission with scholarship. Achu loved studying economics and he was constantly analyzing the three -isms of government—capitalism, socialism, and communism—and how these governments define the production, distribution, and consumption of goods and services, how it impacts the individuals, businesses, government and nations and how choices are made to satisfy the needs to get maximum output. He was supposed to be experiencing democratic socialism in India, but because of the great rift between the rich and the poor, they were not able to get maximum output. In fact, the whole process was not working properly. He wanted to learn more about communism in China and Capitalism in USA.

Achu sometimes picked up his sister from the women's dormitory and go for a walk in Trivandrum. It was a very beautiful city with remnants of the successful Travancore Kingdom. Now it is the capital of Kerala State with assembly building, Kerala University Headquarters, the zoo, the museum, and many government buildings. They used to talk about their childhood, how poor they were, how many days they had nothing to eat, and how they shared a small room in a hut with the grandparents. Because of their academic achievements, both of them were able to stay in better places, but they are aware that the rest of the family is still living in poverty. Achu told his sister that the only way they get out of poverty is through getting good education and advised her to focus on the studies to continue to get scholarship for higher studies.

Final exams were over both for Achu and his sister, and together they went home for summer. He noticed that their landlord had now become a politician. Achu told him about the plans to get admission in Indian Institute of Management for a master's degree in business administration if he could get a scholarship. The landlord told him that his brother-in-law is a professor in Indian Institute of Management and that he would help Achu.

Results were out. Both Achu and his sister were rank holders. Once again, journalists came to interview them and their pictures were published. It was a great story: the children of a poor farmworker family were first rank holders in SSLC and BA Economics from Kerala University. Just like Achu, admission and scholarship were guaranteed for Achu's sister. Achu was offered scholarship for MA Economics in Kerala University. Achu applied for admission with scholarship at Indian Institute of Management. With the help of the landlord, his application was processed and got a letter of admission and scholarship for MBA program. Achu's dream came true. The whole family was happy.

Achu went to thank the landlord. The landlord told him that when he goes to Bangalore, he should let him know so that he could accompany him. Achu's parents were very happy to hear that there was somebody to accompany Achu and help him in Bangalore.

Meanwhile, since Achu's younger sister had passed SSLC with distinction, she also got admission in Kerala University with scholarship. Achu's parents could not believe what was happening to their children, and they were happy and sad at the same time—happy because the children were getting good education for free and sad because they would be leaving again.

Before going to Bangalore, Achu took his sisters to Trivandrum as he promised. His one sister got admitted for a degree in Chemistry and the other was admitted to pre-university program—both with scholarships.

Achu and the landlord went to Bangalore. Achu first met the landlord's brother-in-law and they went to the institute and got settled in the dormitory. This time Achu did not have a roommate—better room and better facilities.

Bangalore is a busy city with more commercial and business activities. He went for a walk near the institute. In the dorm, he met some students. All of them were from different states, and therefore, he had to communicate in English. He was looking around for somebody from Kerala, who speaks Malayalam language. He was thinking about the changes in his and his siblings' lives, all because they are all excellent in the academic field. He was certain that a good career is guaranteed for them. He was happy that the sufferings of his parents will end soon.

CHAPTER 3

Studies and life at the Institute of Management were challenging as well as interesting. Management classes were very informative, a new field for Achu. Achu understood that management studies were basically the tools for administration of an organization, institution, business, or government; management techniques include organizational structure, goal setting, and decision making to have excellent performance.

He learned that there are various levels of management in an organization from top to bottom with varying degrees of responsibility. There are different techniques of management depending on the type of organization and the goals. There is project management, problem solving, time management, personal management, and financial and wealth management. The overall curriculum was very interesting to Achu, and he was thrilled by varying aspects of management. His area of interest was financial and wealth management. He understood that even one's own life can be managed with set goals.

It was June 1960; Achu was 20 years old, a responsible adult. He had to take care of his family as it is the great Indian tradition of the eldest son in the family. He had to ensure that both his sisters get married and his parents have a regular income for old age. His first sister would be completing her bachelor's degree in chemistry in two years. His other sister completed her pre-university course, passed the medical college entrance examination, and joined the medical degree program with scholarship. Achu's parents, who were still working hard to make ends meet, were very happy that all their children are doing very good academically and, therefore, would have bright future.

One of his classmates, Seema Agarwal, used to ask Achu questions while they were in the library. Achu's keen interest in his diligence enabled to provide good explanations to her questions. Seema became his regular companion in the library and, eventually, they started going out in the city together. They became very good friends, and both liked each other's company. Seema's father is a garment exporter, and they lived in Delhi.

Achu and Seema became very close friends, although they lived different lives. Achu was responsible of taking care of his family because of their situation; Seema was the only daughter of the rich businessman. Regardless of their background, they still liked doing things together, either studying or exploring the city. Seema also liked financial management.

During the New Year break, Seema told he father that she was going to visit Kerala and asked Achu to take her. Achu did not want to take her to his place and expose his family's poor living conditions. She already had made reservations to a hotel in Kochi. Achu informed his family that he will be with a friend in Kochi for few days before reaching home.

They spent few days in Kochi for sightseeing the old port city, which was the spice trading center from fourteenth century onwards with Arab merchants from pre-Islamic era. This port was occupied by Portuguese in 1503. After Portuguese, Dutch and British controlled this port, which was under the Kingdom of Kochi. Jewish people from Mediterranean countries migrated to Kochi in early sixteenth century. There were about 2500 Jews. One of the oldest Jewish Synagogue was in Kochi.

Then they went to stay few days in Munnar, the great scenic attraction of Kerala, about 5500 to 6000 feet above sea level. It was created by the British as a resort and for tea plantation. Seema went back to Delhi after spending a week with Achu.

Achu went home. His sisters were there too. They wanted to know about the Indian Institute of Management, his curriculum, and about Bangalore City. Achu wanted to hear about their studies too. His sister told him that she wanted a master's degree in chemistry. He was very happy to hear that. There was no doubt she would be eligible for scholarships.

Achu went to see the landlord to thank him for all the support. The landlord was happy to hear the successes of Achu and his sisters and asked him to bring his sisters so that he can talk to them.

The landlord had become a friend of their family, a total change in the perspective from total dependence to coexistence; what a change the independence and the democratic system of government had done to the society.

Achu's family would get out of poverty because of the academic achievements of the children, but most of the poor still remain poor and the rich remain rich. Achu encouraged all young children in the neighborhood to study better and build a future and get out of being a farmworker for generations.

After the break, Seema and Achu were very happy to see each other again. Seema told him that he should visit New Delhi during the summer break and that they can visit Agra and Jaipur, the two top tourist attractions in Northern India. Achu agreed.

They continued to concentrate on their studies and asked the professors to put them together in projects. One of the projects they received was to study and prepare for the economic impact of the five-year plans of the government of India.

In 1961, India entered the third five-year plan for economic development. These plans were modelled towards Russia's five-year plans. The first five-year plan started in 1951. It achieved a Gross Domestic Product (GDP) growth of 3.6% even though the target was modest 2.1%. National income increased; however, due to rapid population growth and high percentage of poverty, the real growth was negligible.

Agricultural and industrial expansion and establishment of more technical educational institutions were the main goals of the first and second five-year plans. Many lift irrigations systems were established to supply water for agriculture and heavy industries were started. Steel plants were also built.

The targeted GDP growth for second five-year plan was 4.5% and achieved 4.27%, which was good. The country started seeing more employment opportunities and better agricultural production.

The goals of the third five-year plan was to increase national income by 5%, reach self-sufficiency in agricultural food grains production, increase employment opportunity for all citizens, and establish equality among all.

Achu and Seema travelled in the rural and industrial areas of Bangalore to interview government officials, farmers, industrial workers, farmworkers, and students. They gathered their perspective of the past ten years, reviewed reports of the first two five-year plans, analyzed the goals of the third five-year plan, and studied the economic conditions of urban communities and the progress of the country as a whole.

Their paper was so good it was sent to the Government of India, and Achu and Seema received an award. Professors were very impressed with Achu and his commitment to learn more about finance and economics. He had published papers on the pros and cons of democratic socialism in India and the democratic capitalism in USA.

Achu told his professors that he wanted to go for higher studies on finance and economics in the USA. One professor, who had taken his PhD from New York University, helped him make the contact and apply for fellowship after completion of the MBA program. Seema actually wanted Achu to stay in India, get married to her and work with her to run the garment export business of her father.

During summer break, Achu went with Seema to Delhi. Seema introduced Achu to her parents. Mr. Agarwal was very impressed the way Achu talked. He asked him about his plans, said that he wanted to see Delhi, then go to Agra see Taj Mahal and then to Jaipur, Rajasthan. Mr. Agarwal arranged a driver and car for his tour. He asked Seema to make the necessary reservations in hotels for his travel. Achu stayed in a hotel in Delhi.

Delhi has two sections: Old Delhi and New Delhi. The national capital of India is New Delhi. Old Delhi was the capital of several empires of ancient India and Delhi Sultanate including the Mughal Empire from 1649 to 1857. The remains of the Mughal Empire is everywhere in Old Delhi. British moved the capital from Kolkata to New Delhi in 1911; in fact, the foundation for the Viceroy's house and other headquarters was laid by then King of England George V and Queen Mary.

Achu was very excited to see Delhi and its historic sites and museums. Seema took him to the National Museum, the Rajghat, final resting place of Mahatma Gandhi, Jantar Mantar built by Maharaja Jai Singh II of Jaipur as an astronomical observatory, and many gardens in Delhi, went around Old Delhi, Red Fort, Presidential Palace and Parliament Mandir (House).

Next day they went to see Agra on the shore of Yamuna River about 125 miles southeast of Delhi. Agra was founded in early sixteenth century to be the capital of Delhi Sultanate, and for some time, it served as the capital of Mughal Empire. The main attraction was Taj Mahal, built by Mughal emperor Shah Jahan as a memorial for his favorite lover and wife Mumtaz in the mid-seventeenth century. The Agra Fort, also called the Red Fort, was built with massive red sandstone walls by Emperor Akbar.

The next day Achu and Seema were ready to go to Jaipur, which required an overnight stay there. Seema's mother also joined them. While traveling in the car with Seema and her mother, Achu and Seema talked about their education together, how they did joint projects and how they met in the library for joint studies. Seema's mother got the impression that they were in love and tried to find out Achu's background. Achu told her that he came from a poor Hindu family and that he was able to get scholarships for his college education because of being a rank holder in every stage. Seema's mother was impressed with his educational achievements but was not happy to hear about his family background. She doubted whether he was the right person to marry her daughter who grew up in high society. Seema became aware of the type of questions her mother was asking to Achu, so she changed the subject by talking about his plans to study in the USA and that she also was interested in him.

They stayed in a nice hotel. Jaipur is a beautiful City, which was founded in 1727 by Maharaja Sawai Jai Singh as the capital of the princely state of Jaipur founded by the Rajputs in the twelfth century. With mostly rose-colored buildings, also known as the Pink City, Jaipur's main attraction is the palace, which is still home to the royal family, the eighteenth century open-air observatory, and museums.

As they traveled back to Delhi, they were mostly sleeping in the car. Next day, Achu went to Seema's house had lunch with them and had open conversation with Seema'a parents.

From Delhi, he took the train to Kerala to go home to his family. It was a very interesting four-day journey. The train passed through various states from Northern India , a Hindi-speaking state with lot of villages. He witnessed various holy shrines of Hindu religion on the shore of the holy river Ganga. The ruins of very powerful kingdoms of ancient and medieval India were also seen. He was also able to pass by Madhya Pradesh in the middle of India (another Hindi-speaking state with largest reserves of diamond and copper deposits, mountains, thick forests, plain land, and desert, then through Andhra Pradesh (a Telugu-speaking area of coastal region with endless paddy fields and other agriculture, rock mountains, and desert). He noticed the poor living situations in Tamil Nadu, a Tamil-speaking state with mostly drylands. Finally, when entering Kerala, he passed by the Sahya Mountains on both sides through the Palakkad pass, and he saw the beautiful plain land with lots of coconut trees, green valleys with paddy fields, rivers, and streams.

Every village passing through from Northern India has a different culture. They dress differently too. Rich and poor live together. There are hundreds of railway stations. Achu noticed people getting in and out of the train. These people talked different languages. Vendors carried cloth bags on head, coffee, tea, and they called out to sell them. The sound of the moving train and its loud whistles was all new experience for Achu, a true experience of life: seeing people and observing them in their journeys.

Everybody at home was happy to see Achu. Both his sisters were home for summer vacation. The first sister just completed her degree in chemistry with rank and ready to start her master's degree course. His other sister was in medical college. Their parents looked weaker and older.

Achu told them that he will most probably get admission for a fellowship in financial management in New York

University. He also mentioned that after the fellowship and training, he will most probably get a job. He asked his parents to stop working at that time and that he will support them. They were all happy and at the same time sad that if he would to USA, they would not be able to see him often. Achu was confident that his sisters will have successful education and afterwards good careers.

Summer break was over. Achu and Seema reached Bangalore, and were happy to see each other. Time has come for the completion of course with project works and final examination.

Meanwhile, Achu applied for the fellowship at New York University Business School with strong recommendations from his professors. Seema told him that her father wanted her to join his business and take over eventually and that she hoped Achu would come back and join her.

After sending the grades, Achu received letter from New York university informing him that he got admission for a one-year fellowship at the University and one-year training in a Bank to be arranged by the university with pay. Even though she was happy to hear that, Seema was sad that Achu would be leaving her soon.

Together they went to Madras Consulate to apply for visa by train. On the way they discussed their future. Seema asked him to marry her after he finish the New York University fellowship and that she would convince her parents for that. Achu said that he loved her and wanted to marry her next year. Finally, they had to bid farewell. Both hugged each other and cried for a long time. They agreed to write letters to each other regularly.

Back home, Achu started preparations to go to New York within three months, he had to join there at end of August 1963. Achu took his parents and sisters to Kochi to get the suits stitched, purchased shirts, bag and other travel materials. They were visiting Kochi and Ernakulam for the first time, after the necessary purchase Achu bought clothes for his parents and sisters also, walked to see Kochi backwater, harbor, Supreme Court etc. This was the first trip for his parents outside of their village and everything was so surprising to them including the first-time train journey. Achu knew that after going to USA, he may not be back at least for two years until he finishes the fellowship and training. On the way back, Achu's father Narayanan told him that he will be twenty-four years old in 1964 when he finishes the fellowship and when he comes back must get married. Achu smiled and shook his head. His father asked him about Seema, and he told him that he would like to marry Seema. His father was silent.

Achu's sisters bid farewell and went back to college. They were very upset that their brother was going away for long time; Achu told them that one day they all will be in America.

Achu went to see the landlord. He was very happy to hear about the achievement of Achu. He told him that if Narayanan and his wife need any help, they should feel free to contact. Achu was very happy to hear that. He used to look at the landlord as a cruel person, not paying his dependent workers enough to make a living.

Achu bid farewell to his neighbors and they were all very proud of him, the first person in the whole village to ever go for higher studies outside India. In fact, a big news came in the newspaper about Achu, his academic achievements and the trip to America to join New York University as a management intern.

Bidding farewell to his parents was not easy. Together they cried for a long time. Parents were happy that he was going to have a bright future, they blessed him.

Achu had booked the ticket on Air India from Bombay to London to New York. He went to Bombay by train. This was another of his first experience in life, passing through customs, showing passport and visa, go through security clearance, and finally entering the flight. He got a window seat. It was an early morning flight.

Looking through the window, he saw the rising sun. He thought about his childhood of poverty, starvation and difficult life, he thought about his parents, sisters, neighbors, and landlord. They are all now proud of him. He cannot fail them. He must achieve his ultimate goal: become a great investment banker in capitalist America.

He was served Indian food on his flight from Bombay to London. Flight was good. The two guys sitting next to him were always talking in Hindi and, therefore, he could not talk to them. They had to get down in London, go through transit, and enter another flight to New York again passing through security. It was all a great experience.

This time he got an aisle seat. This time they served western breakfast: omelet and sausage. He liked it and thought what type of food he will have to eat once he reaches New York.

His professor had given instructions that once he arrives at Kennedy airport, he would go through immigration where his visa paper would be examined and issued a three-year student visa, then he collects the luggage, go through customs and when he comes out, there would be somebody standing with a sign saying "Welcome, New York University." The professor also advised Achu to talk slowly so that people would understand him and sometimes he may have to repeat what he says.

Achu saw a person standing outside with the sign as said by his professor. He went toward him and said, "I am Achu Narayanan."

He replied, "I am David Johnson, foreign student coordinator from New York University."

Achu did not understand him much, but heard New York University and concluded that he was there to take him. David took is luggage and walked towards the parking lot, opened the trunk of the car, and put his luggage, opened the door for him and then took the driver seat.

Everything was like a dream to Achu. As someone who grew up in a poor farmworker family, seeing that a white well-dressed person taking his luggage and opening the door of the car, made him wonder: Was it real? Was it America?

Looking around he saw hundreds of car parked. David drove through the three-lane divided highways. Hundreds of cars and other vehicles were passing on both sides. Reaching closer to Manhattan, he saw huge multistory buildings. All of it were new experiences for Achu.

David asked him, "Have you been to New York before?"

He quickly answered no and continued, "In India, cities do not have these types of high-rise buildings and multilane highways. It is a new experience for me."

David was impressed with Achu's straightforward answer. They entered city roads, which are narrower and busier, lots and lots of cars, traffic jam and slowing traffic. Achu never expected anything like this. He had been to Delhi, Madras, and Bangalore, no comparison of New York to those cities.

Finally, they reached New York University campus, a beautiful campus in downtown Manhattan, the economic capital of the world. Achu could not believe that he had reached there, a dream come true. Met with the graduate admission office, completed necessary paperwork for 1-year graduate fellowship in Banking and Finance and got admitted to one of the graduate residential halls with free boarding. He would receive $1000 per month fellowship. He is also eligible for two-year training afterwards in a bank or another financial institution.

Achu was taken to his new room with basic facilities, a bed, study table, and chair, closet, and bathroom. He was so tired, took a bath and went to sleep.

After waking up, he went to the office to find out how he can write letters to India. At that time there was no direct phone calls possible to India, only through trunk booking and that is if you have a telephone number at the other end. He had few dollars with him, went and bought couple of International envelopes and stamps, wrote three letters, one to his parents, one to his sisters and one to Seema, just told them that he arrived safe, got a place to live at the university and that he missed everybody.

CHAPTER 4

Next day Achu saw some students in the lobby, looking around saw an Indian-looking person, went up to him and introduced himself, "I am Achu, from India, joined here for graduate fellowship."

The other person said, "Hi, I am Krishna Murthy, last year joined here for MBA program."

Achu was glad that he met somebody from India who had been here before so that he could get more information about the place and the university. Murthy and Achu walked to the street. They lived in Washington Square Village five minutes' walk from Washington Square park, close to underground subway stations that connect New York City with mass transit railroads. Murthy explained everything to him. Being a vegetarian, he explained about the type of food available and also told him about the practices of the residential hall where men and women mingle. Achu had read about and prepared himself on how to behave and converse. Murthy told him that there were few Indian students and that he would introduce them later.

Achu met with the dean and discussed his fellowship responsibilities. He had to take few courses on Finance and Investment in first semester. Second semester he should teach an undergraduate course and also would be assigned a project on a specific area, which need to be completed by August 1964, end of the one year fellowship. Afterwards he would be given opportunity to apply for one year on the job training in a major bank or financial institution and he would get a salary, which would be extended for another year or would get a job there. Achu thanked the Dean; he was now set for next three years.

He wrote again to his parents explaining program and that he may not be able to visit India at least for two years.

Fall semester started first week of September 1963, Achu registered for four courses, in International Banking, Investment Banking, Global economy and financial management. Everything was new experience for him; there were class lecture and minor project assignments. He had to spend lot of time in the library. He was very interested in all four course subjects and the minor projects assigned in the class. He started spending lot of time in the library.

He got a letter from Seema and contents made him very sad. Seema had written that she expressed her desire to marry him, but her mother told her father that he was a lower caste Hindu and came from a poor background. Seema tried to convince them by saying that Achu was studying in USA and she also wanted to go there to be with him. Her parents decided that she should marry their friends' son and help them with the business. At that period of time, it was very difficult for a daughter to defy the wishes of the parents. They wanted her to stay in Delhi.

Achu wrote back to her that since she was the only daughter to her parents, it would be difficult for them to let her go to USA and therefore advised her to forget her wish to get married to him and that he had no plans to come back to India and work. He explained that being a lower caste Hindu coming from a poor family, the customs in India would not permit their marriage and that she was better of getting married from the same caste and also to a rich person. He was not happy to write to Seema a letter like that, but he knew the realities of life.

Achu received a letter from his father saying that because of heavy rain, life had been very difficult. Achu wrote back and said that he would send them money regularly by saving from his fellowship and that they should stop working in the farm.

Achu loved the subjects International Banking and Investment Banking. International banking is transaction between banks in two different countries; these services are often used by multinational companies for commercial banking like money transfer, loans, and overdraft in multiple currencies. Investment banking is creation of capital for government, companies, and other institutions and in the process reorganize, broker trades and conduct mergers, and acquisitions. For global economy and trade, International and Investment banking are key elements. It helps businesses to expand and grow. He studied and read a lot in the library about these subject areas.

One day, Achu was in the library, and he saw an Indian-looking girl sitting few feet away from him. She looked very beautiful. She was also looking at him. He approached her and asked her name. She said her name was Radha and that she was from Madras. She was in New York because her father, an Indian Foreign Service officer and was a member of the Indian mission to United Nations. She was an undergraduate student majoring in Finance and Economics.

Achu explained his background and the current situation. Radha lived with her parents near the United Nations office in an apartment; she had a younger sister who was attending UN high school. She took the subway train every day.

Achu promised to help her with the assignments and expressed a wish to travel in subway. He had heard about the underground subway system in New York connecting all five boroughs of New York: Manhattan, Bronx, Staten Island, Brooklyn, and Queens with underground stations everywhere.

Achu also wanted to see the Statue of Liberty. Radha promised a tour of the subway and other interesting places on a Saturday or Sunday when they had no classes.

Radha one day came to Achu's residence and asked him whether he cooks Indian food. He said that he eats American food now because he did not know how to cook Indian food; he did not know where he could get Indian grocery. Radha promised to bring him some Indian food and also offered to help him cook. Achu was very impressed with her simplicity and affection.

As promised on one Saturday morning, Radha came to Achu's place with poori and potatoes for breakfast. Achu was so happy. After a long time, he was getting some Indian breakfast. They went out together, took the subway to midtown Manhattan to see Times Square, Broadway theatres, then took the ferry from battery park in downtown Manhattan to Ellis Island and Statue of Liberty.

They talked a lot about their family. Achu grew up in the State of Kerala with mother tongue Malayalam, Radha grew up in Tamil Nadu with mother tongues Tamil, both were non-Brahmin Hindus. Radha's father was a self-made Indian Foreign Service officer and mother was a housewife. They became very close friends. After the tour Radha, promised to come the next Saturday and make him dosa and sambar, typical southern Indian breakfast.

Radha often met Achu in the library and got his tutoring on subjects where she needed help. Most Saturdays they met. Radha used to bring stuff to cook Indian food for Achu.

One day Achu told her about Seema and how her parents refused to get her married to him. He asked Radha whether he will have that problem if he wishes to marry her. Radha was speechless for some time. Then she told him that she loved him. She was sorry to hear about his previous disappointment and that if he wishes she would be happy to get married to him. They held their hands together, hugged each other, and kissed. It became a very emotional moment for Achu, he went through it once and was very disappointed. He cried and said that he was very happy that he found somebody to love and be loved and that one day they could get married.

One day he heard that President Kennedy is coming to New York. The young charismatic John F. Kennedy became the president in 1961, who called for a new deal and a new frontier, asked for new laws and reforms to eliminate injustice and inequality in USA. There were people lined up in both sides of the street to see the popular president. Achu and Radha also were there, they were excited, seeing an American President for the first time.

A month later on November 22, 1963, Kennedy was assassinated in Dallas, Texas. America was mourning on the death of a young energetic great President. Achu and Radha remembered when they waited with crowd in New York City streets to welcome this great American president. It was a great experience.

Fall semester ended before Christmas. Achu received A grade for all four courses. There was one-month break until the spring semester started on the last week of January.

The Dean gave Achu some assignments in the office and told him that during spring semester he had some teaching assignments on the subjects he learned. Most of the free time during the New Year break, he spent with Radha, went around several areas in the other boroughs of New York City and surroundings. He saw small neighborhoods in

Brooklyn, Queens, and Bronx where people of a specific ethnic background lived in an area. He saw the American melting pot in New York City, people from all over the World with many ethnic backgrounds and culture.

In Manhattan, he saw the people living in luxury, cars flowing through the streets nonstop, even lot of people walking through the streets of New York after midnight. The nightlife in Times Square and surroundings is why there is a saying, it is the city that never sleeps.

When he got free time, he wrote to his parents and sisters about his experiences and also about Radha. His sisters were curious to learn more about Radha. He wrote them more about her and that he liked her even though she was not a Malayalee. They asked for her photograph. He told Radha about it and she promised to give him one.

In the spring of 1964, Achu had a different experience. First time in his life he was teaching undergraduate students the subjects, International finance and global economy, and his dean also gave him a project to study Global economy in the perspective of Democratic Socialism in India and Democratic capitalism in USA, which he had to submit on August 1.

He was constantly preparing for the class and researching in the library for the preparation of project paper. Radha still gave him company, sometimes cook Indian food for him and they went out often in the City.

One day he visited Radha's parents in their apartment. Achu talked for a long time to Radha's father, who had a master's degree in Economics before passing the Indian Foreign Service exam. He took advantage of the conversation to learn about Indian economy in a democratic socialism. Achu asked him to help him get more information in that area to help complete his project paper and Radha's father, Ramanathan, told him to see him whenever he needed some clarification. Achu was very happy that he met Mr. Ramanathan, and he thanked Radha for taking him to see her parents and younger sister.

Achu started working on his project paper, and he decided to learn more about Democratic Capitalism, since the global economy in the 1960s was led by USA. Capitalism means money. Wealth and goods are privately owned and distributed and therefore financial market is controlled by privately owned corporations and institutions.

The founders of United States when they created the constitution stressed more on the rights of individuals, declaring equal justice, life, liberty and pursuit of happiness and freedom of expression or free speech. It allows individual freedom, take risks for a better opportunity, explore new ideas and dream big. The founders designed a democratic system of government with liberty and justice for all and this democratic system was further defined by President Abraham Lincoln as government of the people, by the people, and for the people.

In this democracy, economic freedom also is included without much of government interference or control and that is what transformed into democratic capitalism. In a democratic socialism, government has control over everything including the production of goods, services, wealth, property, and trade.

In democratic socialism, government seeks economic justice. In a democratic capitalism, there is always conflict with economic justice. That is why one set of ideas are called conservative often identified with republican party as less government and the other set of ideas are called liberal identified with democrats as more government.

Democratic socialism is also called liberal ideas with more government interference. In global economy there are democratic capitalist governments like USA, democratic socialist governments like India, authoritarian governments like China and USSR and so also one-party system like

Singapore. Natural resources like oil, gas, minerals, etc., also determine the economy of the country.

In the global economic indexes, the Gross National Product (GDP), commerce and value of each country's money are separately considered. It is about economic activity between the countries in financial terms and trading of goods and services. For individual countries it is about balance of trade, economic condition of its people and market value of its currency. Achu had lot to learn and understand and he was very excited about the project assigned to him.

Spring semester was over. Achu had to continue to work in the college and work on his project to complete by August 1. Radha had no classes during summer months and was looking for some part-time work in the college. Achu talked to the dean and got a part-time job for her.

They decided to make a trip outside of New York City and go to Niagara Falls. They took a bus from New York City. New York City is at the southeastern end of New York State and Niagara Falls is at the northwestern end border with Canada.

The bus ride was very exciting, passing through the beautiful hills and valleys of New York State, sometimes through thick forests and vast farmlands. They passed through several Cities, Albany, capital of New York State, Syracuse, Rochester and finally Buffalo. They stayed in Buffalo and next day took the tour to the falls, very excited to see the falls of which he learned about it in middle school as one of the Seven Wonders of the World never imagining that one day he will be able to see it.

Radha and Achu enjoyed their trip, and their friendship became stronger. Radha was about to enter her senior year to complete the bachelor's degree program. Achu had reached the final step of his internship that he was looking forward to, complete his project paper and join a major international bank as a trainee in International Banking and Investment.

Radha told Achu that his father would get a new assignment next year to another country. Achu said that after completion of his training, he most probably would get a good job and that he planned to visit India in between. Radha suggested that it will be a good time for their wedding. Achu agreed.

CHAPTER 5

Achu submitted his project paper on July 31, a very detailed analysis of Democratic Capitalism in USA, Democratic Socialism in India and a perspective on Global Economy. That was a July 1964 perspective, which is much different now.

Achu concluded that for a country with lot of resources, wealth, fewer poor people and an old democracy rooted in liberty and equality like USA, Democratic capitalism works; but for a country which was under British colonization for 150 years, a country formed uniting more than 500 small kingdoms, a feudal society, fifty percent of the people live below poverty level, a recent Independent democratic country, like India, Socialism is a better choice.

In a global economy, there are developed, developing, and underdeveloped (third world) countries, the developed countries will always have upper hand, developing countries compete with these countries to expand their trade to increase the value of their currency while underdeveloped countries need aid and assistance from other rich nations.

He commended the role of International Monitory Fund (IMF) of their work in global monitory cooperation, international trade, and secures financial stability for poor nations and World Bank on supporting sustainable projects in developing and underdeveloped countries to reduce poverty.

Achu concluded that the capitalist countries like USA, who encourage investment in innovation and technology has an advantage over socialist countries like India, who invest more on elimination of poverty, increase public health, and educate the mass. He also concluded that IMF and World Bank shall expand their activities to increase economic growth in the third world. The dean was very impressed with his paper. He recommended him for one-year training with possible employment afterward in Chase Manhattan Bank, a leading international bank.

Achu was so happy. He wrote to his parents and sisters about the new developments. Radha heard the news and congratulated him. Achu was thinking, he had such bad childhood, a poor family trying to survive, starving often, five people living in a two-room small hut in somebody else's property, and the parents worked hard to make both ends meet. He attended the local primary and high schools in rundown buildings. His determination and hard work helped him reach where he was now. Achu wanted to build a house for his parents.

His other sister finished her MS degree in chemistry and got a job to teach in the university. Younger one was completing her medical degree in another two years. Look where they have reached living in poverty and despair. All because of hard work and determination of all three children.

Achu wanted to visit India once the training was completed before joining for employment. Before that he had to save money to build the house for his parents. He had promised Radha that he will marry her next year during his trip to India. Lots of plans. Achu hoping that everything will come true. So far, all his wishes have come true.

Achu joined Chase Manhattan Bank, in their branch in Wall Street, Manhattan, New York City, where the American Stock Exchange is. He was an intern in International Banking and Investment. He was reporting to the vice president of International Banking. Achu was at the center of Global Financial headquarters.

Wall Street is where American Stock Exchange is located. He had lot to learn from scratch the banking operations and decided to take maximum advantage to fulfill his ambition to be a player in the global economy. To learn about global economy, he needed to study the resources of each country, its currency, economic status, trade, production, distribution and consumption and figure on how to efficiently utilize in International investment.

In a free market economy like in USA trade is mostly unregulated, and in a socialist country, the trade is regulated because the resources are limited. In a global trade, it is credit transactions through International Banking. Investment is the utilization of the capital for creating additional income or profit.

For international investment, first there is need to identify a commodity or a country, where the investment will produce profit. In 1960s, the global trade and investment was not that popular and because of lack of technology, it was not easy to provide the service. American trade was mostly with Europe.

Lyndon Johnson, who was the American president and was the vice president of John F. Kennedy, sought to build a great society by speeding up the economic growth in USA. Increasing international trade was an important aspect of this economic growth, especially export of farm products. Achu studied this deeply and helped the bank invest in farm products trade. Chase Manhattan Bank always invested in oil production and trade.

Achu and Radha often met, and their recent conversations were about their wedding and future plans. About the time when Radha graduates, her father would be transferred as Ambassador to Singapore, and they all would move there.

Achu had taken an apartment in downtown Manhattan when he started the internship. It is a studio apartment. Achu said that they can stay there initially after marriage and when he saves enough money could move to a bigger place, he was now helping his parents build a better house and also prepare for the wedding.

Radha said, according to their custom, the wedding has to take place at the bride's place and therefore they have to plan it in Madras. One day Achu visited Radha's parents to discuss in detail their future plans. Ramanathan told him that he had to start his new assignment in Singapore on July 1, 1964, and therefore the wedding could be planned in June.

He would plan for Achu and his family members to stay near their house to attend three days of wedding ceremonies. Achu wrote to his parents and sisters about the wedding plans in June 1965, and they were very happy to hear the plans.

He also heard the good news that his first sister is planning to marry one of her colleagues in the college faculty and the other sister will complete her medical degree program and join internship. Achu told all these good news to Radha and said that after their wedding they will have to attend her sister's wedding.

Everything seemed to be like dream to Achu, three children in a working family with no land or proper house grew up in extreme poverty, struggled hard, focused on their education and where are they now? Was it real? How did it happen? How did they get this opportunity when millions still struggle in India to make a living? Is it luck? Is it God's grace or is it destiny?

There were only few more months to finish his training period and Achu was offered a regular job as an assistant vice president in International Banking and Investment, which he accepted and promised to start after July 4 weekend.

July 4 is the American Independence Day. He planned the trip to India end of May, started shopping gifts for his parents and sisters. Radha was getting ready for her graduation ceremony in May after which her family wanted to go to Madras, arrange for her wedding and end of June to go to Singapore.

Everything was planned for Achu and Radha. They couldn't wait for that big ceremony and life together afterwards. Radha also needed to get an internship to extend her visa in the United States. Achu would be sponsored by Chase Manhattan Bank for a permanent visa. Achu got an internship for Radha in Chase starting July. Everything was set for them to continue their life as married couple in United States.

Time has come for Radha's graduation. Her family and Achu attended the graduation ceremony and reception afterward. Radha's father got relieved from his assignment at Indian Mission to United Nations.

Radha and family left for Madras, India. Achu was there at the airport to see them off. In two weeks, Achu completed his training program and went to Kerala. Achu's parents and sisters were very happy to see him; he looked different, taller, and bigger, western-style dressing using more English words while talking.

Achu looked around and saw the new three bedroom house with facilities that his father built with the money he sent, he told father that he liked the house. They talked for two days. Achu told them about two years of his life in United States. How was the University, how was the internship, about

New York City, how he met Radha, about Radha's family and their plans to get married. His sister told about her boyfriend and their plans to get married in June.

They discussed with parents and decided to hold Achu's wedding second week of June and his sister's wedding beginning of the fourth week of June. After consultation between the parents and the respective families, both weddings were fixed; Achu's wedding at Adayar, Madras, to be hosted by Radha's parents and his sister's wedding to be hosted by his family.

Next few weeks were very busy. Achu gave gifts to his parents and sisters and then went to see the landlord to give him a special gift.

The landlord was very happy to see him, a very sophisticated soft-spoken young man, much different from the Achu he knew before. Achu gave him a set of pilot pens; he was very happy and asked him to tell about his experiences in USA. Achu explained everything and also told him that the wedding of him and his sister were fixed; he told him about Radha and her parents. The landlord thought, what a transformation from a farmworker poor family totally dependent on him to a situation that Achu is marrying an ambassador's daughter. Tears ran down from his eyes. He said to Achu, "God gave you and your family all these blessings. You father is an honest man. He worked very hard for me. Never complained. Always thanked me for the support. I have a son, who did not even complete his college." Achu held his hands and expressed thanks for all that he had done for his family and invited him and family to attend his sister's wedding locally.

Everybody was preparing for two weddings. Achu had brought bags for travel, suit to wear and other necessary stuff. Second week of June, Achu and family went to Madras by train. Radha and her father had come to receive them at Madras Central Station, built during the British rule. It was a huge terminal station.

Achu's parents and sisters were there for the first time, all new world for them. Achu's parents and sisters were happy to see Radha, a very beautiful young girl. They were taken to a small hotel in Adayar. There was one more day for the wedding. Radha came and took them for a tour of Madras City next day.

They took a ride through Mount Road, went to Harbor area, where the old British town was developed and also the harbor. They went to see the government museum established in 1851 by the British (which highlights the significance of South Indian culture) several galleries and children's museum, Valluvar Kottam (the popular monument of the Tamil writer Thiruvallu), Fort St. Georgetown (which was founded in 1644 as the headquarters of East India Company), Alamparai Fort (which was erected in 17th century when Mughals were ruling the country), San Thom Cathedral (which was supposed to be constructed over the grave of St. Thomas by Portuguese in 16th century), St. Thomas Mount where St. Thomas was assassinated, Marina Beach, and Connemara Public Library (which was established in 1896).

In the evening, they went to Radha's house, a beautiful contemporary house, all decorated for the wedding. Many of the family members and friends were assembled. The initial ceremonies were conducted by the pujari and after that meals were served.

During social hour, Achu talked to many of Radha's family members, most are well-educated and placed in good positions. Achu also proudly talked about him and his sisters. Achu's parents could not speak much because they neither speak Tamil or English. May of the guests noticed that, and Achu explained to them that his parents were farmers (instead of farmworkers) and they never attended school. Some of Radha's relatives made some wild comments about it and Achu acted like he did not hear those comments, but he was hurt.

Next day was the big ceremony, the actual wedding. Achu put on his American-made suit. His parents had regular Kerala dress and his sisters had nice silk sarees for the occasion with flowers on the hair. Bride and groom were seated, and the ceremony was conducted.

After the wedding, there was a huge reception attended by top government officials, politicians, industrialists, and religious leaders. Achu's parents sat in a corner and observed everything. They could not communicate at all, Achu felt bad and often came to them and introduced many of the guests by pointing to them, not talking to them. Achu's sisters were socializing with many women at the reception.

After the reception, Achu and Radha went to stay at Connemara Hotel, an old British-built hotel. His parents and sisters went back to where they stay. They were talking how lucky Achu was. He could marry a beautiful American educated girl, daughter of an Indian Foreign Service official. Achu's parents were not that happy, they felt that she was not the right match for their son as she belong to different culture, speak different language, and also belong to high society. They wanted him to marry a simple village girl.

Next morning, Achu's parents and sisters visited Radha's parents for the final ceremony with the newlywed. That night, they took the train to Kerala. Achu and Radha went to the station to see them off and told them that they will come next week. Achu and Radha went to see an MGR Tamil movie. MGR or M. G. Ramachandran was the most popular film actor in Tamil and was a Malayalee by birth.

For two days, they went and visited some of Radha's relatives and also had conversations with her parents about their future. They also booked their flight to USA from Madras on June 30. They went to Kodaikanal for the honeymoon. Kodaikanal is the most famous Hill resort in South India in

Didigul District in Tamil Nadu about 7000 feet above sea level established in 1845 by the British.

They stayed there for two days, then went to Trivandrum, Kerala where Achu had is college education. They went to see the famous Sree Padbhanabha Temple, which was still owned by the Travancore King family where billions of dollars' worth of gold is kept, went around to see the clean and beautiful Trivandrum City, went to see Kerala University Headquarters, Kerala Assembly building, etc.

Two days later they went to Achu's house. His parents and sisters were waiting for them, hearing that Achu and his wife were home, all villagers gathered in front of their house, all poorly dressed.

Radha asked Achu who they were and he explained that they were his neighbors and some of them are his parent's relatives and friends. Radha was annoyed and refused to greet them. Achu finally convinced her that she had to greet them all with smiling face and that she could not ignore them because they are poor. Achu's parents and sisters were upset with the situation.

They had arranged one bedroom for Achu and Radha. Radha told Achu that night that she did not want to stay there too long and want to move to a hotel until his sisters' wedding. Achu told her that it did not look good and they had to stay there until the wedding day and after that, they would be going to Madras.

The day before the wedding, meals were served for all relatives and neighbors. The wedding was at the temple where both parties arrived. After the wedding, a reception was arranged in the temple hall.

In the evening the newlywed went to Trivandrum. It was the last night for Achu with the parents before going back to USA. They talked the whole night. Achu told them that he was overwhelmed with all that happened in his life and his family's life. His parents also felt the same way. Everything was like a dream.

All of his relatives in the village were still poor, and he was thinking how they could help them. Achu told his father that when he starts making money, he would develop some projects for them for their economic advancement. Next day he bid farewell to his parents and younger sister promising that he would be visit again within a year or two.

Achu and Radha took the train to Madras. On the way, Radha complained that she did not like the stay in his house that she was not used to such conditions. Achu told her that if she saw the conditions how he grew up, she would not even talk to him and also told her that education is the most important gift one can have.

Born poor was not his fault, but his ambition was to become rich using the capitalistic opportunities in USA. He told that that he did not appreciate her attitude to his relatives and neighbors because they were poor. He told her that once they start living together in New York City, they would face lot of issues, and she should be prepared.

They reached Radha's parents' house. In couple of days, they had to leave for USA. According to Tamil custom, Radha's parents bought lot of steel utensils for Radha, along with other items, and packed them in a nice box. After they leave, her parents and sister would leave for Singapore. Her sister got admission in a college in Singapore. They all went to see them off at the airport.

Radha was crying. She never lived away from her parents. Achu told them that they may visit them in Singapore next year. Achu and Radha reached New York and came to the studio apartment. As they unpacked everything, they realized there was not enough space to put everything. Radha told him that they should move to a bigger apartment soon. Achu agreed.

CHAPTER 6

Achu and Radha started their family life in the small studio apartment in downtown Manhattan. Achu joined Chase Manhattan Bank as an assistant vice president. Radha was supposed to start her internship within two weeks. They went and purchased some western clothes for Radha. They wrote letters to their parents about their new life and job.

In the evenings, they went around walking in New York City. Sometimes they visited Battery Park at the tip of Manhattan from where you can see the statue of Liberty, sometimes to Canal street and Chinatown, sometimes to Brooklyn Bridge connecting Manhattan and Brooklyn crossing east river, which was commissioned in 1883 at that time the longest bridge in the world, 1595.5 feet long and 127 feet above water with six lanes of roadway, elevated train, pedestrian and bicycle lanes. Sometimes they go around New York University and Washington Park where they have old memories. Sometimes they walk up to SoHo, the top shopping center for designer boutiques, where fashionable crowd gather and there are some nice eating places. Sometimes they take the train to Times Square and walk around the Broadway Theatre area. They were very happy together. Radha worked in a different branch of Chase Manhattan Bank nearby.

Achu had a lot to learn about Investment Banking. It was about creating capital for entities and underwrite the debt or equity securities. They also provide guidance on issues regarding placement of stocks. They also evaluate the company's worth when a client wants sale, acquisition, and merger. They also help companies to prepare documentation for the Securities and Exchange Commission to go public. During public offering of shares, the Investment Bank may buy all or most of the shares and often makes profit by selling it later.

Achu's job was very challenging. Often he was involved with International clients and involved in International Banking also. Radha had a regular bank job and being trained for a manager position. Both leave work around the same time and return home about the same time.

Months passed by. One evening when they were having dinner at home, Radha told Achu that she got a letter from her mother. They are doing fine, and enquiring why they haven't moved from the studio apartment. Achu got little irritated; he told her that they need to save enough money to pay the security for the larger apartment and for furnishings.

Radha insulted Achu by saying that she was not used to living in congested spaces and that Achu might be used to it as a person grew up in a small hut. Achu got very upset with her insult, and told her to stop making such comments hereafter and also asked her to tell her mother to stay out of their affairs. They got into an agreement on this; Achu did not complete his dinner and went to sleep on the sofa. Later Radha apologized and they slept together that night.

After few months, Radha was complaining about dizziness, and they went to see the doctor to find out that she is expecting. They were very happy, immediately wrote to their parents and siblings the good news. Achu now knew that time had come to move to a two-bedroom apartment. They located a nice apartment in SoHo, leased it for a year with option to renew, furnished, and moved in.

That night Radha was very happy and told Achu that she understood the difficulty of leasing a bigger place and the high cost in New York City. Many months went by, and Radha took her maternity leave, and her mother came to help them with the delivery and to take care of the baby. Achu was happy that she came even though he knew that she would interfere with their family life.

It is 1966, Achu had become busier at the job. American economy was growing very fast. Dow Jones industrial average, which is a measure of the stock market, topped 1000 for the first time, market was booming. There were several mergers and acquisitions, expansion of manufacturing industries and high-tech electronics. Achu got many opportunities to expand the bank's business and increase the profits.

One night, Radha got labor pain. She was taken to the hospital. A boy was born, both parents were happy and also the grandmother. Grandmother wanted to name him Nathan after Radha's father. Achu wanted to name him Narayan after his father. Finally they named him Narayan. Radha and her mother were not happy, but Achu ignored them.

Once the baby and mother came home, Radha's mother stopped talking to Achu. Achu did not know how to deal with her, one day he told her that if she could not talk to him, she could not stay with him. She stayed for two more weeks and went back to Singapore. Achu was relieved, explained to Radha that the custom in Kerala was to name the first boy after the husband's father; she did not want to discuss the matter anymore. Achu told her that he got a big raise and bonus, and that Radha did not have to go back to work.

Months went by, and the baby was growing up. Sometimes they went out with baby for a walk in the area. They sent the photographs to their parents.

Time had come for Narayan's first birthday celebration. Achu invited some his colleagues and Radha invited some of the colleagues of her father at Indian Mission to United Nations. Achu helped Radha cook food. It was the first time they have invited guests to their house. Some of Achu's colleagues had small children. They all spent a nice evening together and decided to invite each other.

Radha one day asked Achu whether they could go to Singapore for a week and that she missed her parents and sister. Achu said that they could probably go at the end of the year (1967) when he can take few days off during Christmas and New Year.

In the meantime they got a letter from Radha's father informing that he is selected to be in the Indian delegation to United Nations 1967-68 General Assembly which starts in September and that he would come with his wife for couple of weeks. Radha was very happy and Achu also was happy since he did not have to make a visit to Singapore in December. If he they go they had to go to Kerala also. Now he could plan a visit to Kerala next year (1968), when Narayan would be 2 years old.

Radha's parents came. Ramanathan saw the grandson for the first time, and he was excited. They stayed with them couple of nights before the Assembly started and then moved to the official residence provided by the government of India. Often during the day, Radha took the child to her mother and spent time there.

Her mother was not happy with Achu and every time she saw Radha would ask her how her husband was. "Is he still a cheap guy? He cannot think big because that is the way he grew up."

When Achu came home Radha told him that they need to decorate their house better and furnish with expensive furniture. Achu knew why Radha wanted all those luxuries—it was because her mother was influencing.

One day Achu said that if she did not like the way they live she can go and live with her parents. Next time, Radha went to see her mother, she did not come back and decided to stay overnight with them. Achu got very upset and went to their residence and told Radha's father that his wife is a bad influence on Radha. Ramanathan initially did not understand. Achu explained what was happening and how his past poverty was mentioned to ridicule him all the time. Ramanathan understood the situation and told him that he was sorry and that it would not happen again. After 10 weeks Radha's parents went back to Singapore and invited them to visit next year while visiting Kerala.

The 1960s was a golden age for America in terms of economic growth and a tumultuous year: Civil Rights movement lead by Rev. Dr. Martin Luther King, John F. Kennedy assassination was on November 22, 1963, Lyndon Johnson became the US President, Vietnam War, signing of the Civil Rights Act by President Johnson on July 2, 1964, assassination of Malcolm X on Feb. 21, 1965, assassinations of Martin Luther King and Robert Kennedy on April 4 and July 6,1968 respectively, Riots in 1968 after Martin Luther King assassination, anti-Vietnam war protests in 1968, Ricard Nixon becoming US President in 1969, and man landing on the moon on July 20, 1969.

There was no cable news or 24 hour TV news in those days. Achu had very little time to read newspapers, even though he was aware of all the things happening, he was not emotionally involved in any of those incidents except the man's landing on Moon. Achu and Radha had gone to Singapore and then India in April 1968 to visit their parents. They went around seeing

Singapore, an island nation which was the center of maritime trade to Southeast Asia.

British ruled over it for many years, during the Second World War Japan took over the island, but after the defeat was taken back by British. British allowed self-rule in Singapore in June 1959. In 1963, they created a Federal agreement with Malaysia and North Borneo became an independent republic on August 9, 1965. It is a one-party democratic rule, with strict rules and governing. During British times early 1900s lot of Malayalees were employed there for office work while Tamil were hired for labor. However, many Malayalees after retirement settled in Kerala.

Tamil is now one of the official languages in Singapore along with English, Chinese, and Malaya. It is a very clean country with high economic status. There is one main island and 63 small islands.

From Singapore they went to Kerala, India. Achu's father and mother were happy to see little Narayan. Radha still had an attitude from her superiority complex and was misbehaving with Achu's family. Achu noticed everything and ignored it to avoid conflicts.

In 1970, Achu got promoted to Vice President for International Investment, Narayan was three years old, and Radha wanted to go back to work. She found a job in Citi Bank; put Narayan in day care during the day.

Months passed by, and Radha told Achu that they have to buy a house and car that Narayan will be ready to enter kindergarten school. Achu agreed. They debated whether they should buy in New Jersey, which meat lot of commuting time or in Queens, which meant subways for commuting. But from New Jersey, which means both have to commute at least hour and half each way to and from work.

They decided on Queens, bought a beautiful four-bedroom colonial house, and moved in there within a month.

They admitted Narayan in the pre-school. Life became busy, daily commenting to work, picking up child from school, cooking, the normal routines of a young married couple.

Years went by. They had another child, a girl, born in 1972, almost six years younger than Narayan. They named her Padmini. Time had come for Radha to go back to work. They decided to get a live-in maid. Radha's parents arranged a maid from Tamil Nadu. Her name was Jaya, she did not speak English, only Tamil, which had become hard for Achu to communicate, so they taught her basic English to communicate, how to use the phone and their telephone contacts. Radha did not have to cook. Jaya cooks\ed good southern Indian vegetarian food. If they wanted non-vegetarian, they would go out and eat.

After President Johnson, a Democrat, Richard Nixon, a Republican became the 37th President in 1969 promising a new era. He ended the Vietnam War in 1973; afterwards ended military draft for young American Citizens. For the first time a US President visited Communist China and established relationship and signed the bill creating US Environmental Protection Agency in 1974.

But after his reelection in 1974, a there was an alleged break-in by Republican Party operatives into Democratic Headquarters in Watergate Hotel and that President Nixon covered up the incident. It became a big scandal resulting in impeachment investigation by US Congress. Nixon resigned on August 9, 1974, before being impeached. Vice President Gerard Ford became the 38th President, who pardoned Richard Nixon.

In 1976, Georgia Governor Jimmy Carter, a democrat defeated Gerard Ford and became the 39th President of United States. Jimmy Carter took over after the 1973 Oil Embargo by the Arabs after the Israel invasion of Palestine and faced with lot of economic problems like high inflation and interest rates.

In 1979, during the Iran revolution when Islamic Leader overthrew Shah of Iran out of power, on November 4, the radical students took over US Embassy in Tehran and took US Embassy workers as hostages. The attempt by US Military to rescue them was not successful. Carter was defeated by Ronal Regan, a Hollywood actor, and former Governor of California in 1980. When Regan took over as the President on January 20, 1981, the Iranian Hostages were released.

Achu made lot of bonus from the bank because of his high performance. They decided to move from Queens to a suburban town in New Jersey. They bought a two million-dollar mansion in Princeton, the home of Princeton University, a town surrounded by farms, able to get direct train to New York City.

Achu had become Executive Vice President, now he had to travel a lot for expanding the investment banking; his area was India, China, and other Eastern countries. Radha decided to stop working and stay at home. Achu's parents have become old, his second sister who is now a doctor had married her classmate, both his sisters had two children each. Radha's father became Indian Ambassador to Canada. Narayan was 14 years old, studying in eighth grade and Padmini was 9 years just entered third grade.

Achu was selected to go with a delegation to a conference in India on foreign investments. He went with representatives from other banks and industries. They stayed as government of India guests in Delhi.

After the first morning meeting, while going to the dining hall Achu heard a familiar voice calling him from behind. "Achu". He looked back, who was walking towards him. It was Seema, looked the same. She held his hands and with tears coming out of her eyes, she said, "Where were you all this time? I wanted to contact you. Finally you are here in front of me. What a surprise."

Achu also was really surprised and said that he had been in USA working in Chase Manhattan Bank and now a member of the delegation from US. Seema also was attending the same conference. Seema kept holding his hands, weeping and said that she lost her husband two years ago due to a fatal car accident. They have a girl who is 15 years old and that she had been alone. Her father died and mother was still alive and she was taking care of their business. She kept holding his hands. Achu told her that he would be in Delhi for three days and he should be going to Kerala for few days to spend time with his parents and then go back. Seema invited him home; he declined and said that he would be visiting Delhi again soon.

After the conference, the third day, Seema came to his room and spent the whole day with him. They talked about their life in Bangalore and the times spent together. Seema told him that she still loved him. Achu said that he still had love for her, but he is married with two children. Seema told him to be in touch and that she needed him as her friend. They hugged and cried together.

Achu left for Trivandrum in the evening, met with his sister's families and then went to see his parents. He saw them becoming old and weaker. He told them to sell the house they live and that he would purchase a condominium in Trivandrum near their daughters. They agreed. Achu bid farewell to his parents, told them to take care of their health and contact the daughters whenever they need help.

On his way back, before taking the flight from Trivandrum to Delhi, Achu mentioned his sisters about purchasing a flat in Trivandrum for the parents to live. They promised that they would help sell the house in the village and buy a flat in Trivandrum for the parents. Seema came to see Achu again while he was in Delhi International Airport for overnight stay before the early morning flight. Seema told him that she wanted his friendship and love again. He kept quiet. They spent lot of time together in the hotel room. Achu left saying that they would meet soon again. Seema was happy to hear that.

CHAPTER 7

Achu had become a rich person, who conquered US Capitalism that was the dream of his life. A child born in a very poor farmworker family in Kerala, India, living in a two rooms hut with mud floors in somebody else's property, studying under the light of a kerosene lamp, starving often, walking four miles to high school, not enough clothes to change and looking towards a horizon beyond which there was no hope to reach.

Achu now is the product of good education in a socialist country, opportunities and hard work in a capitalist country and working ambitiously for a bright future. Studying Socialism and Capitalism was his harem, now he had experienced both. He had more than enough money to lead a luxurious life. His children were admitted to Princeton Academy, a high-end private school. His wife had become a socialite and philanthropist.

It was an amazing transformation for Achu in 40 years. He could also help his family back in India and improve their quality of life. He had established a hospital in Trivandrum ran by his sister and her husband. His other sister and husband had become professors at the University. His parents were living happily in a luxury condominium in the capital city, very different life than they led in the village as farmworkers; they were enjoying their old age.

Radha's father had retired from the Indian Foreign Service and now settled in Madras, India. Their other daughter was married to a young Indian Administrative Service officer. Everything looked perfect for Achu and life also was built perfect around him.

Beginning of 1980s was an economic disaster in America. Ronald Reagan became the president in 1981, who believed in the theory of supply side economics, which is opposite to demand side economics. To create a supply side economics, huge tax cut is to be given to individuals and corporations, reduce regulations to help manufacturing factories and increase production, abundant supply of consumer goods at lower prices and ultimately will reduce the unemployment.

There was deep recession through 1982, agricultural exports declined, oil prices gone down, and tight control was imposed by Federal Reserve Board on money and credit. Regan convinced congress to pass hug tax cuts, reduce discretionary spending and increase military funding. He was elected for a second term with a landslide.

By the end of Regan's second term, inflation was reduced from 12.5%in 1981 to 4.4% and average GDP growth was 3.4%. Aside from economic growth, there were huge foreign policy successes; he challenged the Soviet Union finally reaching the collapse of USSR. He asked then Russian President Gorbachev to tear down the Wall separating East and West Germany.

Achu used to make trips to India regularly, mainly Bombay, where Chase had investment in offshore oil exploration. Every time he was in India, Seema used to visit him and stayed with him couple of days. For the first time in their life their love and friendship resulted in physical relationships. That was unexpected. Achu felt guilty. He understood that their love still existed. He did not want to continue the relationship. He explained to Seema that he was happily married to Radha and that he did not want to continue the relationship.

Seema did not say anything first. She was upset, then said that she could not live without his friendship. Seema wanted to visit USA soon to look for admission for her daughter in an American University. Achu could not say no, he said that he will be there to help. Seema was happy, then asked him to send sponsor letters for the US visiting visa, he could not say no again. They departed wishing to see each other soon.

In 1984, Achu's son Narayan graduated from high school. He was the valedictorian (rank 1) in the school. He had high scores for SAT also. Radha's parents visited them from India to celebrate the graduation; it was their first visit to the new house in Princeton, New Jersey.

Narayan joined the prestigious Georgia Institute of Technology for Information Technology degree program and he was now staying in the dormitory in Atlanta, Georgia. Daughter Padmini was in 6th grade. Radha's parents toured several places and went to see some old friends in New York City.

One Saturday, while they were talking in the living room, Radha felt dizzy and fell down on the floor. They called 911 and took her to hospital. Everybody was worried; Radha was unconscious for several hours.

Doctors admitted her to do tests on Monday and Tuesday to see what was wrong and what might have happened. Test showed that she had a tumor next to her brain on the left side, they suspected cancer. Everybody was worried, they informed Narayan, who came next weekend to see the mother. Doctors scheduled eight weeks of radiation treatment.

Achu was very worried, was happy that her parents are still there to help. They applied for extension of their visa. Simultaneously Achu created paperwork for their permanent visa application and made Radha sign the documents. A perfect life now had turned upside down. Padmini was upset, but she was happy that grandparents were not going back to India.

Because of radiation, Radha lost her hair. Now she was home resting and most of the time sleeping. Radha's mother cooked nice southern Indian food.

Weekdays Achu was mostly in New York; if late he stayed there often.

One year passed, Achu did not make any trips, Radha had partially recovered, but weak. One day Achu got a letter from Seema saying that she and her daughter were coming to New York and that her daughter Yamuna got admission for MBA at New York University. Achu rented a studio apartment for a month in downtown New York City for them. Yamuna got admitted and took a place in the residential hall.

For Achu and Seema it was time together to talk about their time together in Bangalore, their love started there, lot of memories, almost 20 years passed. Seema said that she sold their business, her mother was old and staying in their house in Delhi, somebody was there to help her. Seema and Achu spent lot of time together in New York City remembering their past love life.

Meanwhile, Radha's condition was worsening. He told Seema bout Radha, she wanted to visit her. Achu told her that it was not a good idea. Seema went back after a month saying that she would come back soon and asked Achu to visit her in Delhi.

Few weeks later, Radha passed away on March 18, 1985. It was a very sad moment for the whole family. The body was cremated. Lot of friends visited Achu and family and expressed condolences. Everybody was sad, sitting home thinking about Radha.

Achu told Radha's father to postpone their returning plan and stay with them, hopefully their immigrant visa would be issued soon. Padmini was holding on to her grandmother, she was mystified that she lost her dear mother. Few days later Narayan went back to college. Everybody had to get used to life without Radha. Radha's sister was very upset; she could not come from India. Achu asked her to visit soon and offered to send her sponsor letter.

After two weeks Achu went to work. He called Seema and told her the sad news. Seema expressed condolences, but inside her was telling that she will get Achu back. She told him that she planned to visit New York after the winter months.

In 1986, Achu got an offer from Lehman Brothers Financial Services, the fourth largest Investment Bank headquartered in New York formed in 1847. They offered him a $500,000 per year salary as Managing Director and heavy bonus based on investment income. He retired from Chase Manhattan bank after 20 years' service with a huge bonus payment. Achu invested that money in Lehman Brother's mortgage lending services; they were involved in commodities services and brokerage services also. Before joining Lehman, Achu went for a trip to India to spend some time with his parents.

After he left for USA 23 years ago, he never spent any time alone with his parents. Radha's parents were home to take care of everything. Flight was through Delhi to Trivandrum, Kerala. Achu stopped over at Delhi for two days and spent time with Seema. She wanted him to marry her. He said that he would, but had to wait until daughter Padmini enters College.

He went to Seema's house to see her mother; she was sick and weak. She was very happy to see Achu, who was now a rich American, highly sophisticated and westernized in his behavior and conversation. Seema had already told her mother about Radha, who tragically passed away due to cancer. Seema also told her that Achu and she still continued their friendship and that they plan to get married in the near future. She was happy to hear everything and blessed them to have a married life together.

Achu arrived at Trivandrum after two days. His sisters were at the airport to receive him, and this was the first time he was coming to India after he lost his wife. They were sad, but found Achu cheering, not knowing that he had his first love back in his life.

They went to the parent's residence, happy to see his parents Achu started weeping. Everybody followed him. It was an emotional feeling. Achu told them that he and the children were fine, and that Radha's parents were with them. His parents were getting old, but they were happy there. Both daughters visit them often and help them with everything.

Achu told them that he would be there four weeks and that he had several plans. He wanted to build a community health center and a school, from nursery till fifth grade in the village where he grew up and provide free health care and primary education.

He contacted their old landlord and expressed his wishes. He invited them to go there, meet with him and discuss the idea. Achu, parents, younger sister, and her husband went to their village to the landlord's house. He and his wife were very happy to see them. Like his parents, they also had become old.

It was lunch time, first time in their life, the landlord served lunch for them on the dining table. When Achu grew up, they never even allowed him to enter their house. Times have changed, prejudices have disappeared, and everybody was treated equal.

They discussed about the project, a nursery, kindergarten, and grade 1 to 5 school along with a community center with health clinic. Landlord agreed to give the necessary land free.

Achu agreed to put both the names of landlord and his father on the building. Achu said that he would also meet the expenses of construction, furnishing and daily operations, landlord agreed to manage it by forming a committee of villagers and Achu's sister and husband, who are doctors, who agreed to visit the health clinic once a month.

They went and saw the land where it was going to be built, it was not in a normal flood zone, but decided to raise the building foundation couple of feet based on the architect's recommendation. They decided to complete the building, furnish, hire employees within a year and Achu agreed to come for the official inauguration with his children.

After coming back from the village, they decided to visit Cape Comorin (Kanyakumari) and Kovalam beach as a family vacation. Cape Comorin is the southernmost tip of Indian Peninsula where the Arabian Sea and Indian Ocean meet, a beautiful location to see both the sunrise and sunset. There is a temple along with a huge manifestation of Parvathi, virgin goddess according to Hinduism, both at the tip built on the rocks. There is a fort built in the 18th century.

Kovalam beach is the most famous beach in India, the most visited by tourists. It is an isolated beach shaped like a half circle and the land is surrounded by tall coconut trees. They spent two nights in Cape Comorin and two nights in Kovalam beach.

It was very exciting times for everybody, first time they were having such a family vacation, they heard from Achu all his experiences from College till now and about his ex-wife and children. They asked him what his future plans were, he told them that he was changing the job, joining a big investment firm as soon as he got back in US. They asked whether he planned to remarry, to their surprise he told them that he would marry his friend while he was studying in Bangalore, whom he wanted to marry at that time and her parents did not agree because of his poor background. He told them that her husband died of a car accident and that she had a 19-year-old daughter who was now studying in New York. He also told that they used to meet at Delhi whenever he visited India and that he would marry only after his daughter Padmini enters college. They were surprised, but were very happy; they told him to have the wedding ceremony at the famous Sree Padbhanabha temple in Trivandrum.

Time had come for Achu to leave. He bid farewell and said that he would be back within a year to open the community health center and school at their village and asked them to visit the site within six months to see the progress of construction.

He took the flight from Trivandrum to Delhi; Seema was at the airport to receive him. Seema joined him in the journey back to USA, since she had to attend the graduation of her daughter earning an MBA degree. Seema stayed in New York. Achu went to Princeton; he had brought lot of stuff from India including gifts for his in-laws and children. Achu participated in the function for Seema's daughter Yamuna's graduation at New York University.

Achu joined Lehman brothers as Managing Director in commodities investment section. That was a tough area, but could create high profits in the investments. Commodities are mostly raw material like crude oil, metal bullions and food products. Then there is futures market like Gold, Silver, and precious stones. Sometimes mutual funds are used to invest in commodities like Oil and Gas by investing in oil and gas exploration, distribution, and refining. The commodities market is often volatile depending on World events, economic conditions, tariffs, inflation etc. Achu initially took training on various activities and company policies. It was tough for him in the beginning, involved in lot of negotiations and travel.

Achu bought a three-bedroom luxury condominium in midtown Manhattan. He often used to stay in hotels in New

York instead of going home; Radha's parents were still there. Achu had requested them to stay with them until at least Padmini graduate from High School. In summertime they would go to India with Padmini for two months. Narayan had a part time job in Atlanta. The construction of the Community Center in his village in India was progressing with his financial support.

August 1987, Achu, his children, and in-laws went to visit India. They went to Madras first; Radha's sister received them, very happy to see them all. This was the first time the children were visiting India after they grew up. They were very excited, went around seeing places.

After one week, Achu and children went to Kerala to officially open the community center. Achu had contacted the landlord, Thomas Varghese, and told him that they were coming after a week and that the official opening of the community center to be conducted. Achu took them to see various places in Trivandrum and spent two days in Kovalam. Children were surprised to see the changes in Kerala, the new tourism places, and other attractions.

Achu, his children, parents, sisters, and their families went to the village in a small luxury bus; they took a hotel in the nearby town Alleppy. Next day they went to see the landlord, who was making the arrangements to officially open the community center. The landlord received them happily, gave them a sumptuous lunch. Achu talked about his childhood and told his children how his family was dependent on the landlord for work, money, and food. He also told them that the landlord was very supportive when he went for higher studies and always wished him and family well.

They discussed the plans for the inaugural ceremony, the landlord; Thomas had become the local MLA (Member of the State Legislative assembly) of the ruling party. He had invited the Kerala State Chief Minister of the State, the Member of

Parliament, the District collector and the Panchayat (a body of several villages in a District) president to attend the function and Chief Minister would cut the ribbon. He had constructed a large tent outside the building and a stage.

It was a Saturday morning, sun was bright, and wind was blowing. A beautiful two-story building with raised foundation with the background of backwaters was visible while Achu and family arrived at the location. Two names were engraved in the front, K. Narayanan and Thomas Varghese, the old farmworker and the landlord in feudal Kerala respectively.

They went inside the two-story building, downstairs the school and health clinic and upstairs the community center auditorium, very impressive building, met with the employees who were doing various functions. While they were waiting, Thomas Varghese and family came.

Lots of villagers started coming and the meeting was ready to start. Chief Minister and other political leaders along with K. Narayanan, Thomas Varghese, and Achu were seated on the stage.

Meeting started with the Indian National Anthem and a prayer song. All guests spoke high of Thomas Varghese and K. Narayanan, the great transformation of the society and especially the success of Achu, who could support the center financially. Achu pledged financial support for the operation of the school, health clinic and community center and also introduced his sisters, their husbands, and his children.

The lighting of the lamp and ribbon cutting ceremony were conducted. Villagers made big noise as a sign of support and happiness. Achu and his family mingled with all the villagers.

Narayanan and his wife were very emotional; villagers were hugging and congratulating them for the great achievements of their children. Achu thanked the political leaders for their participation and the Chief Minister asked him to visit him before he returned to USA, which he accepted.

Achu's children Narayan and Padmini were surprised with the crowd and their appreciation of their father and grandparents. It was a very happy and historic occasion for the village. The village had changed a lot; there were roads and bridges connecting all island villages.

They stayed one more night at Alleppy and went back to Trivandrum. While Achu was in Trivandrum, Seema came and stayed at the Mascot Hotel, the famous hotel originally constructed by the British. She went back after two days hoping to meet soon in New York.

After spending few more days with the parents, Achu and children went to Madras. After couple of days they along with Radha's parents went back to USA.

CHAPTER 8

New school year started. Padmini was in high school. Narayan was in the senior year for his engineering program. He went to Atlanta second week of September 1987.

Achu was busy at work in Lehman Brothers. His area was commodity services. Lehman's majority investment was in mortgage services. When Achu joined the company, it was part of American Express securities, which acquired Lehman Brothers in 1984.

Lehman's major commodity services were in crude oil. It also brokered carbon emission derivatives. Achu had to travel to major oil producing countries in Gulf, Venezuela, and State of Texas in USA frequently. Sometimes when he went to Middle East, he used to take a side trip to India to visit his parents in Trivandrum, Kerala, and girlfriend Seema in Delhi.

Seema always was very happy to see him, her mother had been sick on the bed. Months went by, and Achu lived between the Princeton House and New York Condominium. Padmini was taken care of by grandparents.

US Economy was good, but there were serious droughts in 1986 and 1988, big outbreak of influenza in 1987 and 1988, and the huge federal deficits due to historic tax rate reduction to 28% and reduction in capital gains tax. US economy was growing slow. There was a stock market crash on October 19, 1987. US economy grew around 2 percent in that period. President Ronald Reagan challenged the Soviet Union.

On March 11, 1985 Mikhail Gorbachev became the General Secretary of the Soviet Communist Party. To jumpstart the Soviet economy, Gorbachev declared openness and restructuring of the government, but the instability of United Soviet Socialist Republic (USSR) started afterwards. Reagan met with Gorbachev and perused the cold war.

The year 1988 was important. Narayan graduated from the Engineering College. He immediately got a job with Microsoft in Seattle, Washington State. Achu, Padmini and the grandparents were sad that he was leaving far away. Achu knew that Microsoft was a company that was going to grow big and fast, so he was happy that Narayan got a job there. They all went with Narayan to Seattle and helped him get started.

Padmini entered the junior year of high school. Achu made a trip to the gulf countries for business. He also went to India, stopped at Delhi to see Seema, found out that Seema's mother was very sick. Went to Trivandrum, Achu's parents have become old, but still healthy. Sisters and their families were doing well. While in Trivandrum, he got a call from Seema saying that her mother passed away. Achu went to Delhi and participated in the funeral service.

In 1988, Reagan's vice president George H. W. Bush was elected the president of United States. Reagan era ended in January 1989.

By the end of 1989 the collapse of Soviet Union, the largest country in the World, started. Hungary dismantled the border fence with Austria and declared solidarity. Poland and other Baltic states started taking steps to become Independent.

On November 9, 1989, the German Communist Party (East Germany) announced the change in relationship with West Germany and declared freedom for people to travel to west. Same night people of both East and West Germany started breaking the Berlin Wall, and the wall collapsed. This was a great moment in history.

After the Second World War, Germany was divided. There was a division beaten East and West Europe, East Europe being mostly under Soviet control. President Bush even though was a one-term president, lot of events happened during his time.

1990 was another important year for Achu. Padmini graduated from High school with top scores. She was the valedictorian (rank holder) in the school, and she also had almost perfect score for SAT (School Admission Test), which most colleges use as criteria for admission. Padmini got admission for a seven-year medical degree program in New York University. Padmini could stay at Achu's condominium in New York City.

At this item, Radha's parents expressed that they wanted to go back to India and live their quiet retirement life. Achu could not say anything. He was very thankful to them. Achu and Padmini went with them to Madras to settle them. He gave them a large sum of money.

While in Madras, Achu went to Delhi alone and met Seema. He told her about his plans to marry her soon; Seema was very happy, she said that she would like to sell the house and other real estates owned in Delhi and invest the money in America. Achu agreed and promised that he would help her invest the money. Achu said that they could plan to get married during Christmas or New Year time.

Achu went back to Madras. Padmini and Achu bid farewell to Radha's parents, sister, and family. Parents were very sad. Achu told them to visit every year and that he would send the tickets.

Achu and Padmini went to Trivandrum. All family got together to see especially Padmini, an adult now entering medical program in USA. Padmini was excited to see her aunts and cousins, who all speak very good English.

Achu privately told his parents and sisters his plan to marry Seema end of the year. His sister's husband promised to make arrangements at the temple and a small reception. Achu expected to bring Narayan and Padmini for the wedding and Seema might bring some of her family and friends, altogether they expect about 100 people.

Achu and family went to the village where he had built the community center in the name of his father and the landlord. They met with Thomas, the employees running the center and also talked to many villagers. They were all very happy to see Achu, especially Padmini, the American girl, a beautiful young lady. They took lot of photographs. Few Days later Achu and Padmini bid farewell to the family and went back to USA. Padmini joined the New York University, moved to Achu's place in the City. Achu put the Princeton house for sale.

Achu was constantly in touch with Seema for the wedding plans. He asked her to visit New York during thanksgiving week. Thanksgiving is the biggest family get together and celebration in USA, and Achu wanted to introduce Seema and her daughter to his children and vice versa.

August 1990 Iraq invaded and occupied Kuwait. Saudi Arabia was threatened. US was in a mild recession in late 1980s, was not in a position to go into an International war alone. Therefore, US campaigned for UN support for an assault on Iraq by forming a coalition of countries. The coalition forces pushed Iraq out of Kuwait and liberated the country.

On November 5, 1990, Bush signed the Omnibus Budget Reconciliations Act of 1990 under which multiple tax increases including maximum individual tax rate from 28 to 31 percent were declared. Bush had made a famous statement during his 1988 campaign, "Read my lips. No new taxes." he broke that promise.

In November, Seema came to New York City and stayed with her daughter. Achu had asked his son Narayan to come to New York for Thanksgiving. Achu had arranged a special Thanksgiving dinner in a special room in the Marriott Hotel in Times Square.

Narayan had arrived a day before and stayed with his father and sister. He was excited about living in New York City, told them about his job and life in Seattle. He had made few friends at work. There were lot of people with Indian origin in Microsoft and some of them were senior managers.

Everybody came to the hotel; Achu introduced to his children Seema and her daughter Yamuna. Achu told them that Seema and he were classmates for MBA in Indian Institute of Management. They were friends since. Seema lost her husband few years ago. Her mother last year and that she had no siblings, just the daughter. He also said that he wanted to marry her with their permission, hopefully in December in India.

Seema had already told her daughter about their plans. Narayan and Padmini hugged their father and then Seema and Yamuna. They had a beautiful Thanksgiving dinner with all the customary menu items. They had lot of conversations; Achu told his children that Seema and Yamuna would visit them next day.

Friday after Thanksgiving Seema and Yamuna came to Achu's place. They all talked and got to know each other. Padmini was happy that she would have an older sister now in the city.

On Saturday after talking to the children, Achu called Radha's parents about Seema and his plans to marry her on December 10 at Trivandrum with a small ceremony at the temple; he also invited them to join. They were not happy about it, especially they worry about Padmini. Achu assured them that Padmini would be taken care off and that Seema had a daughter working in New York City after graduating MBA from New York University. They thanked Achu for the invitation and said that they would try to attend the wedding at Trivandrum next month. Narayan went back to his work in Seattle Saturday evening. Seema and her daughter went to India on Sunday.

Achu arrived at Trivandrum on December 8; everything had been arranged by his sisters. They were disappointed that Achu did not bring the children. Seema, her daughter, few family members, and friends arrived at Trivandrum on December 8. They all stayed at Mascot Hotel.

Achu and his sisters visited them on December 9 at the hotel and explained the program for December 10, morning 9 AM wedding ceremony at the temple, after that everybody supposed to meet at the auditorium at Mascot for lunch reception. They expected about 100 people for the reception.

Achu's parents were sad. They knew that their son achieved everything in life, but he lost the mother of his children. Achu told them that the children were grown up now. They met Seema in New York City, and Seema would treat them like her children.

Next day ceremonies went well, and the reception also was excellent. Day later Achu and Seema took her daughter, family members, and friends to Kovalam beach. After spending a day there, they took them to the high ranges of Kerala to see the scenic beauty.

After couple of days, everybody went back. Seema and daughter were living with Achu and his parents. Seema and daughter did not speak Malayalam; therefore Achu's parents could not communicate with them. They visited both sisters. Everybody was happy for Achu; Seema was very friendly with them all.

After couple of days, Achu, Seema, and Yamuna went to Delhi. There they met with some real estate agents and made arrangements to sell Seema's house and some other property that belonged to her parents.

After Christmas, they went back to New York on December 28. Padmini was very happy to see them. She finished her fall semester and now off for a month. Now she has Seema permanently with them. Yamuna stayed separate in her rental apartment. A new life started for Achu and Seema after their college days.

In January 1991, with United Nation's authorization, US formed a military coalition of 35 countries and liberated Kuwait under the war named Desert Storm, which ended in 42 days. President George H. W. Bush became a hero and his popularity went above 80 percent. Saudi Arabia paid $30 billion of the total $60 billion cost. US and coalition forces had easily defeated Iraq and liberated Kuwait from Saddam Hussain. The Iraq war almost doubled oil prices, which increased profit in commodities investment.

Seema's house and other real estate were sold, and she got a big sum of money in Indian rupees. Seema wanted to start a small business in New York City to keep her busy. They decided to open a Indian boutique store along with wholesale supply business. Seema knew lot of designers in Delhi and Bombay. She also had money in India to purchase textiles, hire designers, etc. and also had an export license.

Achu and Seema went to India to set up everything, and start the design, stitching, and exporting operations. They also visited Achu's parents and sisters in Trivandrum.

Achu's father was sick and on bed most of the time. Achu made arrangements for maids to look after his parents. Coming back to New York City, they looked for a place to have store front and storage behind. They found a place on 28th street between Lexington and Park Avenue in Manhattan. Within few months, the store was opened. Indian American population was increasing in New York and surrounding areas. Business slowly picked up, and Seema got busy.

Meanwhile the new Soviet Russian Republic was created. In August 1991 Boris Yeltsin was elected as the President. On December 25, 1991, Soviet Hammer and Sickle flag was replaced by Russian tricolor flag. President George H. W. Bush had a long history with China; he was the head of US Liaison Office in Beijing in August 1974. Bush believed that US-China relationship was critical to the growth of global economy. He had visited China in February 1989 and ever since US-China relationship was growing.

President Bush with all those major events during his presidency could not win reelection in 1992 mainly because of his tax increase that he promised that he will not do, weak economy and a third candidate Mr. Rose Perot, who got almost 20 percent vote. Bill Clinton was elected the 42nd President with 43 percent popular want and carrying 32 states with 370 electoral votes. He was 46 years old, was a lawyer, Governor of Arkansas for 11 years (1979-81 and 1983-1992) and was Attorney General of Arkansas from 1977-1979. His wife Hillary Clinton was a lawyer, they both graduated from Yale law school.

Achu and his family were doing very good financially. Seema's business was building up fast. Achu's bonus payments were in millions every year. Narayan was now a Manager in Microsoft. Padmini had completed two years of her medical program, and Yamuna got a promotion as Manager.

For Achu, his life had become a dream. When he grew up poor, he was happy with what he had, yet wanted to study and wanted to become somebody with a nice job and income so that he could help his parents and family.

When he was in College, he wanted to learn more about democratic socialism in India and democratic capitalism in USA. The socialist India gave him and his sisters free education from where they bounced into good professions, job, and income. Achu went further up with higher education in USA and got into a profession experiencing capitalism in the global financial capital New York City. While Achu's sisters were happy and proud of their profession in India, their growth was limited in a socialistic society, get a good salary, and have a comfortable life.

Achu went beyond having a profession and making good salary. He made huge bonuses and accumulated wealth and his wealth further increased through sound investments, a real product of capitalism. Achu had to face some bad wraps of life. His wife died young and made him a widower, but he was lucky in a way that he had met his first girlfriend accidently, and later he could marry her because she had become a widow. Achu's children were smart and sure to have good profession and comfortable income, but they might not make money like him.

Achu was at the center of capitalism, means creating wealth by all means, surviving in a highly competitive society. He was in a situation where one is at the right place at the right time. Was it one's fate? Or was it because of determination to be there to experience. Achu always wanted to be there and experience the benefits of capitalism that is why he worked hard during his education, his hard work, determination, and ambition paid off. What was next for him? Should he continue to make more wealth? How could he not? His wife Seema also had become a successful businessperson. What else you needed in life? Is money everything in life? When one makes money, goes for more money, like one has fame, go for more fame. Achu always shared his good fortune with his sisters and in community programs in Kerala, India where he was born.

March 1992, Achu got a call from his sister that his father was in the hospital after a heart attack. Achu and Seema immediately went to Trivandrum. When they reached there, he was on respirator. After a day he passed away. Achu cried and was very sad. Achu called Radha's parents and told them about the loss of his father. They expressed condolences and asked about his children. Achu told them that if they were interested to see, he would send them to India, or they could come to New York and be with them for some time.

Lots of people came to visit Achu and family. They took his father's body to the village where he lived. Body was kept in the community center for viewing. His family and friends came. The body was cremated following Hindu traditions. Achu collected the ashes to be thrown in River Ganges for his mukti (salvation).

Seema, Achu, his mother, sisters, and family went back to Trivandrum. On the way, they talked about their life as children in the village, how Narayanan worked so hard to take care of all of them, how difficult life was, and how fortunate they were.

Achu consoled his mother, asked her to go with him to USA; she said that she would live where she was until death.

After few days living with the mother Achu and Seema went to Delhi taking with them the ashes. Achu promised his mother that they would visit her soon with the children. The whole family went to the airport to see them off and wished them all the blessings. Everybody was very emotional.

Seema and Achu as soon as they reached Delhi, took a room in a hotel, cleaned up, and started their travel to Varanasi by car early morning, it is a 560 miles journey, takes about 14 hours through road.

Varanasi was also known as Banaras, the holiest city for Hindus on the shore of the Holy River Ganges in the State of Uttar Pradesh (northern India). Banaras is known for silk and perfume industry. There are about 2000 temples in Varanasi; the most important are two temples, Shiva and Vishnu temples. River Ganges is about 1700 miles long begins at the foothills of Himalayas at Gangori in Uttarakhand State (at that time UP State or Northernmost India), passes through plain lands in the north towards east to Bangladesh and empties into Bay of Bengal. Ganges means river of plains, the holy river of Hindus, drains through one fourth territory of India.

Varanasi is the cultural center for several thousand years; Moghul Emperor Akbar established his headquarters there. Achu and Seema reached there in the evening, so excited to see the sunset and the multitude of people on the shore of Ganges praying and meditating. They had arranged a hotel nearby and checked in there.

Early morning, they got up, dressed for the occasion, took the ashes of Narayanan, went to shore, and then walked into the river with many people around them. Achu holding the ashes and Seema holding his hand dipped in the water and Achu released the pot with the ashes. Achu was weeping; Seema held him and consoled him. They stayed there looking at the rising sun for about an hour. They came back to the shore, visited both the temples, prayed, and went back to the hotel room. Achu called his mother and sisters and told them about the holy occasion, they were very happy, they never thought Narayanan's ashes would be flown in River Ganges. Miracles were happening in their lives.

Achu and Seema went around Banaras seeing places including the famous Banaras Hindu University. From there, they went to nearby Sarnath, one of the holiest places of Buddhists and visited Bodh Gaya. It is believed that Gautama Buddha attained enlightenment under a Bodhi tree. They visited that location also. Sarnath was the seat of Aryan religion and philosophy in 2000 BC. They also went to Allahabad, the largest City in Uttara Pradesh. Allahabad is the meeting pit of three rivers, River Ganges, the Yamuna, and the Sarasvati. Seema's daughter is named after Yamuna. They had a very peaceful and enjoyable time in those places. It was spiritual experience also, sort of a renewal in their life. They both had experienced great loss in their life, which resulted in their reunion. It was all a great turn around

When they came back to Delhi, they visited their business associates, Seema's family members and friends. In January 1992, value of Indian rupee collapsed. It was 20 rupees for a dollar and became 30 rupees, a 50% depreciation in value. It was good for exporters. Therefore, the garment exporters with whom Seema dealt with were happy. Seema stared a non-resident dollar account and rupee account in the bank. They went back to USA after few days.

CHAPTER 9

Mr. Bill Clinton had sworn in on January 21, 1992 as the 42nd President of the United States. He was the first baby boomer president, meaning people born after the Second World War during the post-war baby boom, 1946-1964. The American economy had dropped into recession in 1991, stock market recovered in 1992, federal budget deficit continued, and financial industry had lot of problem. Commodities investment was not making much return, real estate investments also were getting dull.

Achu wanted to retire after his children get married and become independent, before he reaches 65 years old. He was planning his investments accordingly. He had a substantial investment in the real estate portfolios.

Summertime in 1992, Achu sent Padmini to India to spend time with her grandparents and aunties in Madras and Trivandrum. His son Narayan was not interested to go, and he was busy at work.

Meanwhile, Seema's daughter Yamuna informed them that she wanted to get married to her Jewish boyfriend, who also worked in her bank as a manager. They decided to get married in November through a Jewish ceremony. It was a shock for Achu and Seema initially; they got over it, accepted the reality, and agreed to help conduct the wedding. They met with the boy, Robert Cohen, discussed their future plans to move into the condominium owned by him in Queens, New York, after the wedding. His parent lived in Brooklyn, New York.

Achu and Seema visited them and discussed the wedding plans. Jewish wedding ceremony is very different from both Hindu and Christian weddings. Some of the features of Jewish wedding include a Ketubah, which is signed by two witnesses, a Chuppah, a ring owned by the groom that is given to the bride under the canopy, and breaking of the glass. It has two distinct features, Kiddusshin and Nissuin, or dedication and marriage. After the marriage, the wife has to follow the Jewish religious practices. Yamuna was ready to practice the Jewish tradition.

Padmini came back after spending summer vacation in Madras and Trivandrum. She was very happy that she could spend time with grandparents, aunts, and cousins. Madras was hot, she liked Kerala better. She went to watch Hindi, Tamil, and Malayalam movies. She did not know any of those three languages, but she could understand little bit Tamil and Malayalam.

Achu told her about the wedding plans of her stepsister Yamuna; she was very excited to hear that.

Padmini started her fall semester classes. Achu and Seema were busy with the wedding plans. With the help of Robert's parents, they found an elegant banquet place in Queens, started inviting friends and colleagues.

Achu informed his family in Kerala and invited them to come for the wedding. Seema invited her cousins in Delhi. Narayan also was excited about the wedding, and he planned to attend it. Achu's younger sister and husband expressed interest to come for the wedding, Achu sent them invitation and sponsorship. Few of Seema's cousins also were interested to attend and they were also sent the necessary invitation and sponsorship.

Wedding day had come; Yamuna was dressed in Indian Sari, looked very beautiful. Before leaving, they had a minor Hindu Pooja at the house. The wedding ceremony was in a hall next to the banquet hall, about 75 people attended the wedding and about 150 people attended the reception. It was a grand reception attended by many colleagues of Achu from Lehman brothers, Colleagues of Robert and Yamuna, relatives from India and Roberts' family and friends.

After the wedding, Yamuna and Robert went to Bahamas islands for honeymoon. Seema was sad, she felt like she lost her daughter. Achu told her that they would be living in Queens and that she could visit her any time. Achu and Seema took the relatives from India, his sister and husband and two cousins of Seema and their spouses to see New York City, the Statue of Liberty, took them to Niagara Falls and Washington DC, the usual places when visitors from India come.

Achu started going to work in the morning, and Seema opening her Boutique store. Achu was off on Saturdays, but Seema opens her store on Saturdays when she had he maximum business. Saturday, they usually go out for dinner, sometime go for a Broadway theater show. All of Broadway Theatres are mostly in midtown Manhattan, and the shows are musicals. Those shows are very big attraction and for good show hard to get tickets. Hollywood film stars often act in those theatre dramas. Sunday mostly they stayed home; sometimes took a stroll in the Central Park, which was only few blocks from their condominium.

On Sundays, they sometimes would invite friends for brunch and chat, sometimes would visit friends. Some Saturdays, Padmini used to come home to spend time and sometimes Yamuna and husband also would come for brunch. Achu stopped his regular travel schedule; Seema was planning to sell her boutique. Then one day Achu got a call from his older sister telling him that his mother was in the hospital, and her condition was serious.

Achu and Seema left for India by the next available flight. Achu could not see his mother alive. It was too late. He was very upset, cried loudly when he saw the sister at the airport. They went straight to her house, where the body was kept for viewing.

Sitting next to his beloved mother's body, Achu was thinking back to his childhood life. She did not have nice clothes to wear, every day she had to worry about cooking food for the family of five, sometimes nothing to cook, just rice with lot of water like a soup with chili pickle. She never complained, at end of the day very tired and went to sleep on a mat on the mud floor. Woke up early every day and continued the routine again. Life was real struggle for her.

The poor people limited their life within their families and neighbors; they never imagined a life beyond the horizon. Now Achu had become an American millionaire, living in luxury, he could never bring his parents to USA. He regretted it. After all what is life? Life is what you make of it within your resources and taking advantage of the opportunities. Everybody may not get the same opportunity, but education is the best resource for a better life. Achu and his siblings have proved it.

Janaki was the name of Achu's mother. Her body was taken for cremation; Achu had to put the light on the chita (the body put on a wooden pile to cremate). The basis of cremation for Hindus is the belief that by doing so, the body is separated from the soul, freeing it to move towards mukti (salvation). Achu believed that his mother's soul would achieve mukti, an innocent woman, never attended school, but all her three children attained higher education and attained good career. She had seen their success and enjoyed it.

Achu's mind was unsettled; he did not feel like going back to New York City to the artificial life of luxury. He had to do something for his mother, discussed it with his sisters, and they suggested to do something for the women's employment and empowerment. He met with the State Chief Minister whom he met during the inauguration of the community center in the village. As advised by the Chief Minister, Achu agreed to donate money to build a women's center named Janaki women employment training and counseling center. He asked his sisters to work with the Chief Minister's office in establishing the center and that he would meet all the expenses.

Achu called Radha's parents and told them the sad story. They expressed their deepest condolences. They asked about Padmini and Narayan. Achu invited them to New York. They said that if Narayan had plans to get married soon, they agreed to attend the wedding. Achu and Seema left for Delhi and from there to New York.

In 1996, President Clinton was reelected for a second term along with his vice president Al Gore. The second term of Clinton's exhibited the best economic performance for America. Average economic growth was 4.5% with low unemployment. Fiscal and monitory policies helped expand the economy. Yet because of the allegations of having an affair with an young intern in the white house, Ms. Monica Lewinsky, along with other previous allegations of affairs followed by the impeachment by US Congress by the Republican majority in the house of representatives for perjury and obstruction of justice during the investigation of the allegations, the great economic advancement was overshadowed. The Senate acquitted President Clinton.

During the 1990s, commodity market was steady. No big growth in oil, gold, and sugar investments. Achu continued to make is personal investments in real estate services.

The availability of mobile phones to consumers started in 1991, and by 1993 it started becoming popular. Throughout the late nineties the mobile phone development continued. Beginning 2000s, mobile data started developing. Investment in mobile phones during this time was very lucrative. Achu made some investments in mobile phone and technology companies. Seema finally was able to sell her boutique store and wholesale business. She invested her money in safe bonds, did not want to take any risk.

1990s was an eventful year for Achu's family; Yamuna's wedding and the passing away of Achu's mother. Seema's daughter Yamuna was expecting a baby boy, and her due date was in March 1996. Seema was very excited to see the little Jewish Indian boy.

One day, Narayan called Achu and told him that he was engaged to a woman he met in Seattle; she was Chinese migrated to US with her parents, currently working in Boeing as an Engineer. Achu was surprised that he was already engaged and that also with a Chinese girl, yet he congratulated him and asked what his plans for getting married were. Narayan said that he wanted to get married in June 1996 and wanted to have a simple ceremony and reception in Seattle. Achu asked him why he wanted in Seattle; he said that his friends and the girl's family were in Seattle. Achu agreed and told him to make necessary arrangements and that he would pay the expenses.

Achu told the good news to Padmini and Seema. Padmini was very excited; she was upset that her brother never told her about a girlfriend. Of course, he was much older than her. Achu asked Padmini whether she had a boyfriend; she told him that she liked an Indian boy who is a doctor in the hospital where she was doing her internship rotation. Achu hoped she would marry that Indian doctor, but did not say anything.

Achu was very excited that his son was getting married. He called his sisters and asked them to attend the wedding with family in Seattle. They were not very excited about Narayan marrying a Chinese girl and that also Seattle was too far away.

Achu called Radha's parents and invited them; they said that they would attend the wedding in Seattle. Padmini wanted new silk saree from India and asked grandparents to bring her sarees and ornaments. Achu sent them tickets to Seattle and back to Madras. Narayan visited New York to discuss the details of his wedding. He had several options, a Hindu wedding, a Chinese wedding, a Christian wedding or a civil ceremony and he preferred a Christen wedding, which means he had to become a Christian, his fiancé was Christian from Taiwan. Achu and Padmini agreed to have a Christian wedding. Narayan had to accept Christianity and he decided to do that in Seattle. His fiancé, Lilly and her parents used to attend the Presbyterian Church, Achu decided to join the Episcopal Church where some of his colleagues attend.

Little boy was born to Robert and Yamuna, named him Isaac. Seema was so excited carrying the boy, a good-looking child with blue eyes. Padmini was happy to see her little nephew. Achu congratulated Seema for becoming a grandmother.

Narayan's wedding was coming close. Achu, Seema, Padmini and Yamuna and her husband with the child left for Seattle three days before the wedding. They stayed in a Marriott Hotel where the wedding reception was arranged.

One day later, Radha's parents came and took room at the same place. Narayan brought Lilly and her parents to the hotel and introduced them to his family and grandparents. They had dinner together at the hotel and discussed plans for the wedding. Padmini had to be one of the bridesmaids and she had to be fit into the special dress designed for the wedding, there were four other bridesmaids, who were all Lilly's friends.

The day before, the family got together for dinner; Achu was excited and talked about his life from childhood to Narayan, Padmini, Yamuna, and Robert. His childhood memories were horrible: starving days, not enough clothes to wear, and poor living conditions. But his hard work and education helped him become what he was now, and he could help his family also. Achu told them that they were all very lucky, born with silver spoon in their mouth, never experiencing the difficulties in life except Narayan and Padmini lost their mother and Yamuna lost her father early. Achu told them that Seema and he were there for them.

Hearing what Achu was talking, Robert told them that his parents' story were much different. Both his grandparents were born in Germany and were killed by Nazis along with six million Jews. His father who was nine years old escaped into Austria with others, his mother who was 8 years old and some social organizations took them to France. Robert said that his parents, both migrated to USA after the Second World War, met in New York in High School, got married when they became adults and they were very poor living in Queens, New York City.

For Narayan, Padmini, and Yamuna, these stories were great lessons of history. Radha's parents listened to the conversation. Ramanathan loved history. He told them more stories about the small Kings and feudalism in India and how they mistreated the farmworkers. He told them more stories of Second World War, Hitler's atrocities, and how the war was won with America's help. He also told them the role played by Indian Army in the Second World War, which was at that time British Army fought both in Italy and Far East.

On the wedding day, Narayan dressed in black tuxedo, along with groomsmen, five of his friends arrived in the limousine and so also Achu, Seema, Robert, Yamuna, little Isaac, and Radha's parents. Padmini was a bridesmaid. Narayan and the groomsmen entered through the vestibule and waited near the podium The ring bearers, flower bearers, and bridesmaids came in and finally Lilly was brought in by her father holding her hand while "Here Comes the Bride" played. Everybody stood and greeted. The priest appeared in ceremonial clothes and announced that the ceremony, the Holy Sacrament started.

The wedding ceremony was conducted, where two persons enter into a lifelong union, makes the wows before God and the Church, receive the grace and blessing of God to help them fulfill their wows. According to Church the wedding is intended by God. In front of God, both persons promise to love, comfort, and honor and keep the spouse in sickness and health and forsaking all others, to be faithful to their spouses until both are alive. Bride and bridegroom exchanged wedding rings taking this oath. Members of the congregation were also the witnesses. Two people representing bride and bridegroom signed the register in the church along with the new couple and the priest who conducted the wedding.

There were about 150 people for the reception including Narayan's colleagues, boss, and their spouses or friends. Achu and Padmini spoke about Narayan; they both said that he was a serious person and very focused. Lilly's father said that he was very happy that his daughter had married Narayan a smart young man and congratulated both.

Radha's parents were emotional, and Ramanathan wanted to say few words. He said that his grandson had the personality of a diplomat, perhaps inherited from him and that him and his wife was very happy that he married Lilly, a beautiful young girl.

In 1997, Padmini completed her medical program and started her residency at Mount Sanai hospital in New York City for specialization in oncology. Padmini and Rahul decided to get married when her residency completes. Rahul was an assistant professor at New York University Medical College.

Meanwhile, Narayan called and gave Achu the good news that Lilly was expecting. He congratulated the son and asked him to call if he needed any help. Padmini also offered to help.

Achu had one more thing to do before retiring, conduct the wedding of Padmini and Rahul.

In few months baby girl was born for Narayan and Lilly, named her Radha. The grandparents were very happy to hear the good news; especially the baby was named Radha. They were eager to visit to see baby Radha, named after their daughter Radha. Achu told them that Padmini would be getting married to an Indian doctor soon and that he would let them know the date. He wanted Radha's sister and family and also his sisters and family to attend because it would be the last wedding in his family.

CHAPTER 10

Achu was preparing to retire from Lehman Brothers soon after Padmini's wedding. He expected a huge amount as bonus, several million dollars, when he retires. He wanted to diversify the investments; he had invested a large amount in Lehman Brother's real estate services and a substantial amount in bonds and stocks.

Achu wanted to create hedge funds with few of his friends in banking industry and manage it. Hedge funds invest and trade liquid assets; they are traded with extreme use of leverage and more complex investment techniques. They are less regulated investments and sometimes can get huge returns. Hedge funds are considered unregulated alternate investments and therefore it has the ability to make more extensive use of leverage and more complex investment techniques. Hedge funds usually invest in liquid assets and they are less volatile, often make short-term profits, not like private investment funds where profits are expected after few years. Achu had few of his colleagues to join the Hedge fund.

In 1999, Padmini finished her residency and joined the oncology department of Mount Sinai Hospital in New York City. Achu asked her about her wedding plans. She agreed to have a Hindu ceremony since Rahul had Indian Punjabi background and she had Kerala background. They had to plan a combination ceremony with both traditions.

Achu and Seema talked to Rahul's parents who were living in New Jersey. They decided to hold the wedding in the month of May, a two-day ceremony. First day they would follow the Kerala traditions, and the second day, Punjabi traditions for the final wedding ceremony. They booked Sheraton Hotel in 7th Avenue Manhattan facilities for the wedding and reception and also rooms for guests to stay. Achu invited his sisters and family and Radha's parents and sister and family and offered them flight tickets and one or two weeks stay at Sheraton Hotel. They all agreed to come. It was going to become a great family get-together for Achu.

The last two years of President Clinton were the golden years of American economy, Federal budget had surplus for three years, unemployment was low, and inflation was moderate and no wars. Investors also made lot of money. Technology industry was booming, especially the so-called Y2K or Year 2000 scare when the year changed from first century 1000 to second century 2000, how the computer programs will convert the year. Federal government passed huge funding to create protection of computer data and safe transfer to 2000 called the Y2K funding and offered grant to all government and some non-governmental agencies. The scare also had become worldwide; it was a great harvest time for computer programming companies.

Time had come for Padmini's wedding, Radha's parents, her sister and husband, and the 18-year-old daughter who wanted to achieve higher studies in the US. Achu's sisters and family, older one and her husband, the younger one, her husband and her two children all came couple of days before the wedding and checked in Sheraton Hotel in New York City..

Achu had sent them money to purchase decorative materials for the wedding mandapam (stage), gold ornaments for the bride, and special Kerala Kasavu sarees with cream color and golden (kasavu) borders for everybody including Seema, Yamuna, Lilly, Radha's mother, and special saree for Padmini. Radha's parents had brought expensive Kancheepuram silk wedding saree for Padmini and some gold ornaments as gift.

Three days before, Achu had a family get together in his condominium, a great occasion where everybody talked each other, ate and drank together. Food was catered by an Indian restaurant. For Achu, this was the one and only occasion for all his family members to come together and had an enjoyable time, sisters and their families, children and their families, Radha's parents and sister and her family. They talked all day and night; Narayan and family along with Padmini went to the hotel and slept there.

Two days before the wedding, bride and bridegroom's families met Sheraton hotel, where lunch was arranged in the hall to discuss pre-wedding and wedding arrangements. Achu and family were responsible for the traditional Kerala Hindu pre-wedding ceremony on the previous day. They had to create the necessary decorated area inside a circle in the hotel auditorium, make arrangements for garlands, music, and vegetarian lunch.

Rahul's family was responsible for the traditional Punjabi Hindu traditional wedding arrangements. They had to make other arrangements: white horse chariot for bridegroom to come, musical, and dance groups, and grand dinner during reception. They discussed everything in detail. The auditorium was rented for two days and the lunch on previous day and dinner reception on the wedding day were arranged in the banquet hall. It was going to be a very expensive wedding for both families.

Day before the wedding everybody was preparing for the pre-wedding or engagement ceremony. Achu's sisters and their family decorated the special area for the ceremony with some help from the hotel.

For Kerala Hindus yellow is the more prominent color in decorations. Garlands were ordered and a Poojari (Hindu priest) came from the Queens Hindu temple. Padmini dressed in Kerala Kasavu saree and with lot of gold ornaments along with her family members came first. Then Rahul dressed in Kerala Kasavu mundu and silk juba came surrounded by his family. The Poojari was leading the ceremony, bridegroom walking in circles holding the bride's hand and Poojari sang the Hindu mantras (prayer) in Malayalam, the official language of Kerala.

Finally, bride and bridegroom exchanged garlands, lit the lamp (nilavilakku). Bride and bridegroom bent down and kissed the feet of their parents. The ceremony finished, everybody greeted each other and congratulated the bride and bridegroom. Everybody assembled at the banquet hall for a vegetarian meal catered by a South Indian vegetarian restaurant.

On the day of the wedding, everybody was excited. It was in the afternoon. Achu told everybody to take rest and be ready by 2 PM and assemble at the auditorium. Rahul's family was responsible for putting up the Mandapam (stage) for the wedding ceremony.

By 2 PM all family members, friends, and guests assembled at the auditorium. Punjabi Bhangra music group was ready. Padmini, surrounded by her aunts and other women in the family walked towards the podium.

Bhangra music was playing. She was dressed in a red saree with studded decorations, lots of jewelry. She looked beautiful, everybody was looking at her, and she took her seat on the mandapam.

Suddenly, everybody saw the Bhangra music group walking towards the exit door of the auditorium. Rahul was coming in a horse chariot with a white horse. Music was played at high pitch, the hotel guests and people were looking with surprise, Rahul got down and walked towards the mandapam. He was dressed in typical north Indian block printed red silk kurta. All family behind him, Rahul took the seat next to Padmini.

Special Panjabi Hindu Poojari had come, who conducted the ceremony. Bride and bridegroom exchanged ring; gifts were exchanged by the parents.

Achu made a surprise announcement that he had bought a new house for Padmini and Rahul in New Jersey. It was a surprise for everybody assembled. Rahul's parents thanked Achu for the great gift, Padmini, and Rahul hugged and thanked Achu and Seema.

After the wedding everybody assembled for the reception in banquet hall. Achu had invited many of his colleagues and so also Rahul's father. About 300 people were there. Bhangra dance had been arranged. The DJ was playing both Hindi and English music for dance. Everybody was dancing and having a great time.

The day after the wedding, everybody slept till noon. Achu and Seema came to the hotel and invited everybody to join for lunch.

Radha's parents and sister said that they had to visit some friends and go back in a couple of days. Achu's sisters and family will be there for another week. Achu invited them to his house and stay there until they leave.

Narayan, Lilly, and little Radha were leaving the day after. Rahul and Padmini had gone to his parents' house and, from there, were leaving for their honeymoon in the evening to Hawaii.

Achu and Seema went to their house in the afternoon to see off Padmini and Rahul. Achu told them that after they come back from Hawaii, they could order furnishing for the new house. Rahul's father said that he would pay for all the furnishings. It was a huge house in Bergen County, New Jersey, worth about $2 million. Rahul and Padmini were very lucky to have rich parents. For Achu, this was the ultimate gift to her dear daughter, who lost her mother early in her life.

The 2000 presidential elections happened. Republican Candidate George W. Bush, eldest son of 41st president George H. W. Bush narrowly won after recount of the Florida State and involvement of US Supreme Court in declaring the election. He defeated then Vice President Al Gore; Bush's vice president was Dick Cheney. George Bush and Dick Cheney sworn in in January 2001.

When Bush started his presidency, everything was calm and normal. Achu officially retired from his job at Lehman Brothers with a huge bonus, still had most of his investment there. Achu and three of his colleagues, who also retired, created a hedge fund.

Achu also purchased a three-bedroom condominium in West Palm Beach, Florida, as a winter house. Rich people in Northeast USA, like New York, New Jersey, Connecticut, Vermont, Boston etc. usually purchase a condominium in south Florida, where the weather is always warm so that they could go to Florida and live during winter months from December to March. Some of them would permanently move to South Florida once retired from work and business.

Achu wanted to keep his condominium in New York. West Palm Beach is winter vacation place for Canadians and some Europeans also. It is on the west shore of Southern Florida north of Miami, surrounded by lakes with lots of beach area.

In the meantime, Yamuna and Robert had another boy born. They named him Simon. Seema was there to help; Yamuna took a leave of absence from work.

Achu got a call from Radha's sister informing him that her father died of a heart attack and that the body will be cremated next day. Achu expressed his heartfelt condolences and said that he will visit them soon.

Achu and Seema now had a relaxed life. Achu and his friends were managing and operating the investments. Hedge fund usually will not make risky investments. There were symptoms for a mild recession end of 2000 and early 2001. George W. Bush signed his first of several tax reforms in March 2001.

European union also was going through a mild recession. Therefore, the hedge fund did not take off as planned. When Bush started his presidency, everything was calm and normal.

Suddenly on September 11, 2001, the terrorist group al-Qaeda attacked United States. Nineteen terrorists, most of them from Saudi Arabia and others from Egypt, hijacked four planes that took off from Boston and Newark. New Jersey airports, hit the 110-story World Trade Center twin buildings and the US Defense headquarters Pentagon building in Virginia, killed 2997 people, destroyed the twin buildings and some surrounding buildings to ashes and destroyed a section of Pentagon building. Two planes hit the twin buildings, one hit the Pentagon and the fourth one, which was supposed to hit the Capitol was shot down by US fighter planes.

This was the deadliest terrorist attack in human history. America and the rest of the world were shocked. The two 110-story World Trade Center buildings collapsed within an hour and 42 minutes. How did it happen? A group with no fighter planes, no tanks, no military, no ships, attacked the greatest power in the world using its own commercial flights. Military and political leaders of that time were still in shock. New York City economy was significantly affected, American stock exchange was closed till September 17. World Trade Center buildings and some surrounding buildings were in rubbles.

President Bush took the leadership of rebuilding; he came to New York and comforted everybody. The shockwaves of this 9/11 attack was everywhere, and Americans came together in solidarity. United States concluded that al-Qaeda, who were given refuge by the Taliban-led government in Afghanistan, planned this attack under the leadership of Osama Bin-Laden, son of a millionaire construction magnate in Saudi Arabia.

United States and allies attacked Afghanistan on October 7, 2001. They successfully drove Taliban from power and put a civilian president in charge, nearly 300 Americans were killed. The war continued to defeat Taliban completely and established democratic government in Afghanistan.

In December 2001, Achu and Seema temperedly moved to their new condominium in West Palm Beach to avoid the winter months in New York City.

Life was very quiet there. Every evening, they walked in the beach area. Most of the neighbors were older people, nice places to eat, and sometimes go on boat. They got to know some of the neighbors.

One day Achu got a call from Narayan informing that his wife Lilly was expecting and in few months a boy will be born. Achu was glad to hear the news, more grandchildren. Achu told Narayan that they will visit after the boy is born and asked whether he needed any help. Narayan said that Lilly's parents were there to help.

To his surprise, Padmini called after a week telling Achu that she was pregnant. Achu was so happy to hear the news. He congratulated Padmini and Rahul and told them that they will be back in New York in March; Padmini said that she is due in June 2002.

Seema also was very happy. They both would have five grandchildren. What a phenomenon. They can't believe they both were going to be 62 years old. Usually in US people retire at the age of 65; they retired early with millions of dollars in the bank and investments. They planned to travel to places all over the world once the grandchildren were born.

On March 2002, Achu and Seema came back to New York. Yamuna, Robert, and children Isaac and Simon came to see them. Isaac was going to be six years old seen, and Simon was turning two years old that year. They were very happy to see the grandparents. Padmini and Rahul visited them two days later.

Padmini's due date was June 28, and she was expected to take maternity leave end of May. Meanwhile, Lilly was due in April. Achu and Seema were feeling the pressure of these upcoming births of grandchildren. They decided to go to Seattle early May to see the new grandson, told Padmini to stay with them after they come back from Seattle. Yamuna told Padmini to call her if needed any help.

On April 20, Narayan called with the good news. A boy was born, and they named him Albert. Achu and Seema went to Seattle, eager to see the boy, waiting for Narayan to pick them up from the airport. Narayan came, greeted them. Narayan and Achu hugged each other. They got into the car and started the travel to Narayan's house.

Narayan had bought a bigger house in Seattle suburb Redmond, and he told them that recently he was promoted as a director. Achu and Seema congratulated him. They reached his home. It was a huge colonial house. Achu was proud of his son and his achievements.

Lilly opened the door. Albert was placed on a baby seat on the sofa. Narayan had told that the name Albert is English version of Achu, could call him Al. Achu took Al in his hands and kissed him, gave to Seema and she also kissed him and gave the baby to Lilly. It was a very happy occasion.

At night while getting ready to sleep Achu started the conversation with Seema, "We are so blessed. Children are all doing fine, they have healthy children, good job, good income, and good places to live. What else I need in life? I loved my wife Radha, but when I lost her due to illness, I got you, my first lover whom I could not marry. Life is strange, but it is always nice to me. I know I passed thrpugh very bad conditions during to my early life. For some reason ever since I came in United States, my good fortunes started."

Seema replied, "Achu, everything happened because of your good performance in school and college and your hard work. Your children also are very smart. I am also blessed because I got you back, even though it was after a tragedy, which was my fate. We shall continue this happy family life. Achu, you are a good father. My daughter loves you."

CHAPTER 11

After coming back from Seattle, Rahul and Padmini visited Achu and Seema and told them that end of the month Padmini would start her leave of absence and that she would live with them until delivery. Rahul said that whenever he could come, he also would stay with them. Achu asked him about his parents. Rahul told them that they are doing fine and asked to visit them coming Saturday.

In 2002, the economy was fairly good, unemployment was about 6%, and the GDP growth was about 3%. Afghan war was still going on. The Hedge fund was being operated with fairly good profit. Achu did not get involved in daily operations of the Hedge fund. He had about 50 percent of his investment in real estate with Lehman Brothers, 25 percent in stocks and bonds and the other 25 percent in Hedge fund, and then he had some money in savings and got dividends, which he used for his expenses. Seema had all her investments in stocks and bonds. Financially they had no worries.

Achu and Seema were enjoying Padmini's stay with them, they talked a lot every day. Padmini talked about her profession as oncology doctor in Mount Sinai Hospital in New York, the most famous place for cancer treatment. She said that most of the patients did not survive and the difficult part was facing the family members.

Achu used to talk about Kerala, the beautiful place where he was born, but as a child often starving with no food, he never saw the natural beauty of his village surrounded by water, coconut trees everywhere. Most of the people in the village living under poverty. Seema, meanwhile, born to a rich businessman in Delhi, as one child got all the nurture, experienced the luxury, and grew up in the capital city New Delhi.

Padmini asked them the story of their love affair and the reason why they could not get married. Achu told her that they used to meet in the library and to do joint study and projects. Achu said that he left for USA and Seema went back to New Delhi, her parents got her married to the son of his friend, a businessman.

Achu said that he met Radha at New York University, who was completing her undergraduate program, while he was doing the internship. Radha's major was finance, and she was one of the few Indian students at that time in the university. Radha and Achu became friends. She used to cook Indian food for him and take him around for New York City tour.

One day while talking in the afternoon Padmini got labor pain. That night a boy was born. Rahul also came. They were all very happy. Rahul declared the name of the new baby Ajit. Achu was happy that it was another name sounded like Achu. Mother and daughter were brought to Achu's New York City condominiums and after couple of weeks they went to their house in New Jersey. They had now five grandchildren. Luckily they did not have the responsibility to look after them.

Achu and Seema decided to go to India during August-September 2002. They went to Delhi to meet friends and relatives. Then they went to Madras, visited Radha's mother who was with Radha's sister, she was sick on bed, Achu told her about Narayan's second child Albert and Padmini's new baby boy Ajit. She was happy to hear about the new grandchildren.

From Madras, they went to Trivandrum, Kerala. Achu tried to contact Thomas Varghese, the landlord in the village and was told by his son Jacob that he had died five months ago. Achu was sad to hear the story and expressed his condolences to Jacob. Achu told him that he would like to turn over the responsibility of operating the school and community center to the local government and that he would visit the village in few days, Jacob welcomed the idea. Achu transferred the ownership of his condominium to his other sister and established a trust fund in the other sister's hospital to treat the poor people who could not afford to pay the bill.

Achu and Seema went to Alleppy, stayed in a resort hotel, and went to the village. They along with Jacob met with the Panchayat (local government of villages like a municipality) president and other officials and made arrangements to transfer the ownership of the community center.

House boats were getting popular in tourism especially in the backwaters in Alleppy. Achu and Seema rented a houseboat for one night. It was a very enjoyable tour on the backwater surrounded by small islands filled with coconut trees. There were other boats passing by. They served seafood and Kerala rice dinner especially shrimp and Karimean (a tasty fish that mostly lives in the backwaters). At night, the houseboat was docked someplace because of the fishermen.

From Alleppy they went back to Trivandrum, bid farewell to everybody, and took the flight back to Delhi.

Seema always wanted to go to Kathmandu in Nepal located on the other side of Himalayas, the only Hindu Kingdom in the World. Kathmandu is the capital of Nepal with a population of one million, home of the Newar people. They took a direct flight from Delhi. It was a two-hour flight crossing the Himalaya Mountains and then cruising down to the plain to about 4500 feet above sea level where Kathmandu was located on the plains. It was an exciting flight, they checked into a hotel.

Newar people are Indo-Aryan and Tibeto-Burman ethnicities, who follow Hinduism and Buddhism. They are known to contribute to their culture in literature. Trade and agriculture were their primary source of income. Silk and wool rugs were manufactured there.

Achu and Seema went around this magical place. There were lot of Hindu and Buddhist temples, different from Indian cities; people looked like Chinese and Indian. They went inside several temples, and it was a great spiritual experience.

They returned after two days. The flight back was even greater experience going up the Himalayas and then coming down to the plains. From Delhi they returned to New York City.

They went to see Ajit, son of Padmini and Rahul. The baby was only few months old, excited to see the little grandson, spent lot of time with him. Next day Achu got a call from Radha's sister informing him that her mother died, Achu was sad, he expressed his condolences and told her that he would inform Narayan and Padmini about their grandmother's death, who took care of them during their childhood when their mother died. Padmini cried a lot, called her aunt, and expressed her deepest sympathy and regretted that she could not visit while she was sick on bed. Narayan also called the aunt, expressed his condolences, and asked her whether there was anything he could do.

Achu wanted to find a hobby to keep him busy, he never played golf, decided to get into reading and maybe writing. Seema loved cooking and exploring new types of cooking like Italian, Thai, etc.

One day Achu got a call from Narayan saying that he got a new job as the Chief Operating Officer of a new IT company in San Jose, California. He had to move within sixty days and that the new company would make arrangements to move and also provide him a residence to live. Achu was very happy to hear the good news, and he offered any help needed. Narayan said that Lilly might have to quit her job and, therefore, she could take care of the children. Achu wished him all the best and said that they would visit him after he settled down in the new job.

With three children and five grandchildren there would be some news and event all the time. Achu and Seema went to San Jose in early December to be with Narayan and his family. They were settled in a nice house closer to the beach. San Jose is the center of IT. This area south of San Francisco is known as Silicon Valley.

They were very happy to see their grandchildren, Radha, who is now 5 and Albert only few months. Albert looked at them and smiled. They loved to hold him. After spending about ten days with them, they went to Florida to live in their winter home. Every evening they went for a walk along the beach, then sit there looking at the waves, lot of older couple walked around holding hands. Indian couples do not hold hands and often the wife walked 6 feet behind the man.

Seema cooked breakfast and lunch every day. They ate dinner from restaurants in the beach. They did not have a car. either they used taxi or limousine. Achu bought a collection of H. G. Wells books to read.

H. G. Wells was known as the father of science fiction, and he had great influence on English literature. He was born in Kent, England, in 1866, died in 1945 and had written forty books and many short stories.

Achu and Seema came back to New York end of March. On March 20, a US lead coalition of western countries invaded Iraq declaring that Saddam Hussain was hiding weapons of mass destruction and aiding terrorists. Economy roared back in 2003 even though there was an initial slump because of the Iraq war, but the job market did not pick up, interest rates were very low, and therefore housing market was up. Several CEOs were caught for insider trading and other fraudulent activities. Achu was making money on his investments including Hedge Fund.

Achu and Seema were planning for their retired life. They decided to make trips to places around the world during September-October every year. December through March, they would live in the winter home in Florida and rest of the time in New York City. While they were in New York, they would visit the children and their family.

In 2003, they decided to go to South America, Peru, Argentina, Brazil, and Colombia. Bogota, the capital city of Colombia, was the hub of their travel. They took their flight to Bogota, a city at 8660 feet above sea level with a population of about 10 million. It is a beautiful city with hills and valleys, heavily populated and lots of dining places, theaters, beautiful churches, and parks. Columbia is a Spanish speaking coutry. They stayed for two nights at Bogota and flew to Lima, a 3-hour flight.

Lima is the Capital of Peru with population of about 10 million people. It is a desert city on the Pacific coast about 150 feet above sea level that covers about 1000 square miles area with a low population density.

Peru also is a Spanish-speaking country, and the people are very friendly. They toured the Larco Museum which displays the history of Peru's ancient civilization, Plaza de Armas and the 16th-century cathedral. After staying two nights in Lima, they flew to Curso, city in the Peruvian Andes which is 11000 feet above sea level. Curso was the Capital of Inca Empire, the indigenous tribe of Peru. The north of Curso is the Vilcabamba mountain range about 13,000 to 20,000 feet high. Curso is not very heavily populated but a beautiful city with several hilltops.

Spanish colonization of the Americas under the Crown of Castile started in late 15th century. Americas were invaded and became part of the Spanish empire, who invaded most of Americas, except Brazil and British controlled North America. Half of South America, all of Central America, and parts of North America were captured, and the Spaniards invaded most of Caribbean islands also. After Christopher Columbus discovered the Americas and the Spanish invasion, about 80 percent of the indigenous people in those areas were massacred. Same thing happened in North America where the Native Americans known as the Red Indians were killed. It is estimated that about 2 million Spaniards emigrated to Americas between 1492 and 1892 and another 3.5 million to Latin America afterwards.

Achu and Seema had very nice time in Curso. From there they took the train to Machu Picchu. This train trip was perhaps the best journey they ever had. The train with its glass roof, comfortable seats, and restaurant passed though the valleys of Andes Mountains 8000 to 13000 feet high, slowly going up in elevation.

There were Incas residences on some of the mountains and old ruins of Inca culture on some other mountains. The train went side by side with the stream that flows in between the mountains. The train reached its destination at the town called Aguas Calientes, about 4 miles always from the ruins of Machu Picchu. They had made reservation in a hotel there for two nights stay.

Machu Picchu is the Inca Citadel at the top of an 8000 feet high mountain, founded in 1450 and abandoned in 1572 during the Spanish invasion, situated in the southern mountainous region of Peru, which was the estate of Inca emperor Pachacuti. It was not known to the Spanish during the colonial period and the ruins of Machu Picchu were brought to attention by the American Historian Hiram Bingham in

1911. It was built in the classical Inca style with polished stone walls; the ruins were reconstructed and had been restored.

They spent one day visiting Machu Picchu, bus tour took them to the top of the mountain, and they could walk around and see the ruins, it was an amazing scene that would capture your imagination of human spirit. Next day, they went hiking through the beautiful area walking by the side of the river and surroundings. They returned to Curso, stayed there one night, then to Lima.

From Lima Achu and Seema flew to Buenos Aires. Buenos Aires is the capital of Argentina, another Spanish-speaking country at the South-Central end of South America. In Argentina, 96 percent of the people are of European descent, mostly Spanish and Italian. Like all of Americas, it is also a Christian country and like most of Central and South America mostly Catholic.

Buenos Aires is located at the northeast edge of the flat plain known as Pampas, the agricultural heartland of Argentina, about 150 miles from Atlantic Ocean, and it is the center of commerce, industry, technology, and culture. It was a clean city with wide roads. They enjoyed the Argentinian steak dinners and went to the Argentinian Tango Dance Theatre.

From Buenos Aires they flew to Rio de Janeiro, the former capital city of Brazil, a major tourism attraction, the only Portuguesa speaking country and the largest country in South and Central Americas with a population of about 210 million. Brazil is an ethnically diverse multicultural nation because of mass immigration from all over the world during the last century. Again, as all countries, it is also a Catholic majority country.

Rio de Janeiro is the most populous city in Brazil, was the capital of United Kingdom of Portugal, Brazil and the Algarve 1815-1822 and was the capital of independent Monarchy, the Empire of Brazil until 1889 and the capital of Republic of

Brazil till 1960. They took a tour of Buenos Aires, strolled the beach and went to see the famous huge Christ the Redeemer statue built between 1922–1931 created by French sculptor Paul Landowski, 98 feet high, arms stretching 92 feet located at the peak of 2300 feet high Corcovado mountain.

They also saw Casa Rosado, famous presidential palace, Recoleta Cemetery site of art-rich mausoleums, Plaza de Mayo, and Caminto, colorful street and open-air museum. They also took a tour of the rural and desert areas of Brazil. They also enjoyed the Brazilian cuisines, especially the Portuguese-style cooking. They spent three days in Buenos Aires. They decided not to take a tour of the Amazon jungles.

From Rio de Janeiro, they flew back to Bogota and stayed two more nights there. They loved Colombia, especially the coffee shops and the nice Colombian coffee, Colombian food, and the people. They could not speak Spanish, yet they could communicate.

They returned to New York, , took the limousine from Kennedy Airport to their residence in New York City. They called all the children and told them that they were back; everybody had lot of questions about the trip and excited to hear their narration. They had bought gifts and mementos for everybody.

Yamuna and family visited them next day and they went out for dinner. On Saturday, they visited Padmini and family was happy to see Ajit. He started walking few feet at a time.

Life was back to normal. They had to plan their trip to Florida in December. They asked the children to visit them in Florida. Yamuna and husband agreed to visit during Christmas-New Year holidays.

Achu talked to Narayan about the new job, and he was very excited to talk about it. His company was doing very well. Achu talked to his partners in Hedge fund. They reported that the fund was making good returns.

Achu and Seema went to Florida in December. Seema was engaged in experimental cooking. She had bought some cooking books during their South America trip. Achu liked steak both Argentinian and Colombian.

Achu now spent his spare time in reading. He had bought the H. G. Wells collection of books. As before, they went for a stride on the beach every evening and spent time talking to the neighbors.

During Christmas holidays Yamuna, Robert, Isaac, and Simon came. Isaac was 7 years old and Simon was 3. They had nice time together. Children loved the beach. They also went to Disney World in Orlando, stayed there three nights. The children loved the Magic Kingdom Park with live fairytale shows, travel in the space museums, Animal Kingdom with music, Hollywood studios encounter the Thriller, many rides, and water park. After coming back to West Palm Beach, they took a ride to Miami Beach. Children were having such a nice time; they did not want to go back.

Achu and Seema retuned to New York in March. Padmini called them and told them the sad story that she was expecting two months and had a miscarriage. She was sad. Seema consoled her and told her to try again after a year. Padmini told that that the doctor advised that she should not try for some time.

Economy was performing normal in the 2000s, no great job growth, GDP growth was average 2 percent, and the corporate growth was above normal. Both Afghanistan and Iran war continued with lesser intensity.

Achu and Seema were planning their trip to Africa this time. Narayan invited them to San Jose to spend time with his children during the summer vacation. Radha was 7 years old and Albert was 2. They decided not to make a trip in 2004 and spent time with Narayan and his family in California. They bought gifts for the children, packed up for a two-month stay with Narayan and family. It was the first time are going to spend long time with Narayan after he left home for work in Seattle.

Narayan, Lilly, and children were happy to welcome them to their home. They were given a bedroom upstairs. Immediately, little Radha said that she was going to sleep with her grandparents; Albert was too young to recognize them.

one weekend, they went to visit San Francisco, which is about 50 miles north of where they lived. Driving north along San Francisco bay was so beautiful. They went straight to bay area to see the Golden Gate Bridge, a one mile long suspension bridge built in 1937 connecting the San Francisco Bay abovethe Pacific Ocean, and it is 746 feet high. Then they went to the Golden Gate Park, Lombard Street, a steep street, pier 39, walked around and had a nice time.

Achu and Seema were having good time with the children. They all made a trip to Napa Valley, the wine country, which stretches about 50 miles to 100 miles north of San Francisco. They drove through the beautiful area, stopped to see how the wine is made and experienced wine tasting.

Another time they decided to go to Disneyland, the first theme park built by Walt Disney himself. The Disney World in Orlando, which they visited with Yamuna's children was built afterwards, both are similar.

Disneyland is in Anaheim, California near Los Angeles. Los Angeles is about 340 miles south of San Jose. They drove there. Anaheim is about 26 miles from Los Angeles. They had booked hotel in Los Angles for six nights so they could visit Southern California. Two days they spent in Disneyland. The kids loved the rides. They spent lot of time in the adventure park.

One morning they drove to San Diego, about 120 miles south from Los Angeles, border with Mexico. It was a beautiful scenic drive, in fact the most scenic route in the Pacific coastal highway. San Diego is a beautiful clean city, they went around to see the harbor and other scenic areas and returned in the evening.

Rest of the days in Los Angeles, they went to Hollywood, visited Universal studios, Warner Brothers studios, Chinatown, the beach, and one day, they went to Manhattan Beach.

In the area where Narayan lived in San Jose, there were lot of Indian and Chinese families, Narayan and Lilly had made lot of friends.

Achu and Seema visited some of the family friends. They had nice two months with the grandchildren, a great experience, children were upset when the time came to leave, and they promised to come every year and spend time with them and invited them to visit New York City during the vacation time. Narayan also was little upset; he never spent this much time with the father after graduation and also, he got to know the stepmother more. He told them to visit them at least once a year and promised to visit them more often.

Achu told Narayan that life is all about love and be kind, he advised him to be humble with whatever achievements he makes professionally. He said that he always thought about his childhood life in poverty and always ready to help the people in need.

After coming back to New York, they relaxed for few days. Yamuna, Robert, and children visited them; they had brought some gifts for the children. They visited Padmini, Rahul, and little Ajit, who was four now, talking a lot, hanging on grandpa's shoulder.

Achu loved his grandchildren. He always bought them gifts, whenever he saw them, he thought how unlucky his parents were, no money to give gifts, no money to buy clothes and even no money to buy food. His children and grandchildren never experienced poverty, they could not even comprehend what poverty is, another generation born with the silver spoon in the mouth.

Achu knew that he was the person who created such a life for all of them, but his children did not know that. Everything was normal for them. They never faced any difficulties in life; they were very responsible and hard working.

CHAPTER 12

US Economy was smooth during 2004, GDP growth was normal, 3 to 4 percent and inflation was normal. America was stuck in two wars, Afghanistan even after defeating the Al Qaeda, Taliban forces were still there fighting against the Americans and in Iraq also Americans were fighting against the insurgents. Many people blamed President George W. Bush for getting into war with Iraq, since no weapons of mass destruction was found in Iraq.

President Bush was reelected in 2004. He defeated democratic candidate Senator John Kerry. Second term of George W. Bush started in 2005. His main focus was free trade agreements with multiple countries, economy had slow growth; tax cuts did not really help the economic growth. The war against Afghanistan and Iraq continued to cost billions of dollars for Americans even though it was a coalition of several countries that was involved in those wars.

Achu was getting good returns on his hedge fund as other hedge funds. Achu and Seema planned to visit Africa; they took medicines for yellow fever and for malaria, got antibiotics,

Tylenol, and first aid kits. They were well-prepared for the Africa tour.

They stared the trip in June, flew to London, and from there to Nairobi, Kenya, a country in East Africa with coastline in Indian Ocean. Nairobi was not a safe City, they went a tour of the outskirts with great scenic view, went for the famous savanna safaris. After three days, they flew to nearby country Uganda and landed in the capital city Kampala.

Uganda is a mostly Christian country with English and Swahili as official languages. Uganda is a very fertile land, and agriculture is the major source of income. At one time, there was a large Indian population in Uganda. In 1972, then President of Uganda Idi Amin expelled about 50,000 Indians from there. He was a brutal dictator, who also slaughtered more than 300,000 Ugandans.

After spending two days in Kampala, they went to Tanzania by ferry through Lake Victoria, which separates Uganda and Tanzania. Lake Victoria is the largest lake by area, about 23,000 square miles, about 1120 to 275 feet deep. Ferry took them to Mwanza, Tanzania. It was a beautiful journey.

They stayed two days in Mwanza, visited the Saanane Island National Park, a 10-minute boat ride from Mwanza, went to see the Bismarck rock and Sukuma Museum, where they saw displays related to Sukuma culture. Sukuma are the largest ethnic group in Tanzania, about 16 percent of the population and they live in the western and southwestern African Great Lakes region, their religion is animism, some Islam and some Christian. From Mwanza, they went for five days Safari tour package at Serengeti National Park, the world's biggest wildlife refuge. Those five days were the most exciting and relaxing days of the tours they had taken so far, herds of wildlife, all sorts of animals freely walking through those preserved landscapes, breathtaking views. The safari they saw at Kenya was nothing compared to what they saw at Serengeti.

From Serengeti they took the 3-hour flight to Dar Es Salaam, the former capital and biggest city in Tanzania, about 530 miles away on the Indian Ocean coast. They visited the village museum where the authentic and tribal homes are displayed, went hiking at the Udzungwa Mountains National Park and Kigamboni beach. They stayed for two days at Dar Es Salaam and flew to Casablanca, Morocco, a 9-hour flight.

From East Africa, they had come to northwestern Africa, where the ethnicity, culture and tradition are very different. Morocco is at the northwestern corner of West Africa with Mediterranean Sea to the north and Atlantic Ocean to the west, an altogether different landscape. Kingdom of Morocco population is about 35 million, ruled by several dynasties since 788 AD and occupied by several invaders, French, Spanish and mainly Portuguese from 15th to 18th century. Morocco is an Islamic country with official languages Arabic and Berber. Being a member of Africa and Arab unions Morocco wields lot of power and also Casablanca being a port city at the northwestern corner of Africa, there are lots of trades. Spent three days in Casablanca, went to the beach and sightseeing in the outskirts of the city to see the remnants of Moroccan culture. From Casablanca, they took the 3-hour flight to London. They stayed in London for two nights, took rest, and flew back to New York City.

By the end of 2005 economic growth weakened, unemployment was above 5 percent, and the housing market was booming. Achu and Seema were 65 years old now. It was time to join Medicare insurance. Achu decided to withdraw his funds from the Hedge fund, which was not making much return and invest in real estate funds.

Achu was planning his full retirement, eventually moving to Florida and sell the house in New York City. As usual they went to Florida in December and came back to New York in March. The economic and job growth were slowing down in

2006, Federal deficit was skyrocketing due the expenses of two wars, US Trade deficit was growing fast, and oil price was also going up.

Narayan and family were planning to visit New York, and therefore, Achu and Seema decided not to go for any tour this year. The children would be with them throughout the summer to spend time with the grandparents. After the schools were closed, Narayan and family came. The children were very excited; Radha was nine years old and Albert was five.

They took the boat ride around Manhattan, took a trip to the Statue of Liberty, spent couple of days with Padmini; her son Ajit was also five years old. Narayan and Lilly went back after two weeks leaving the children with the grandparents. Achu was so excited to take care of the grandchildren. He asked Padmini also to leave Ajit in New York with them.

Achu hired a Nanny for one month to clean and help prepare food for children. Yamuna's children, Isaac and Simon, also joined them during the day. Achu and Seema often took them to walk in the Central Park; they all went to New Jersey beach a couple of times in a big van they rented and, one time, to the Great Adventure amusement park in New Jersey.

Every evening they went out to get ice cream in central park. The children and grandparents had lots of fun. For Achu and Seema, this was more enjoyable than going for tedious tours around the world. Lilly came to take Radha and Albert back. The children and grandparents were very sad. Achu and Seema decided to have these types of get together every summer. Lilly invited them to California the following year.

The third quarter GDP was below 3 percent and the economy was in a standstill. Housing boom came to an end, debt was building up for everybody, job growth continued to drop, trade deficit widened, and America's dependence on foreign oil increased. Achu was watching the change in US economy, and he did not see any panicking situation but only saw growth as per his analysis.

They took their annual trip to Florida in December and came back in March 2007 as usual. US Economy remained in bloom but never reached a panic stage. This year, they planned a trip to the Far East. Seema had never been to that part of the world even though Achu had been to Singapore, Hong Kong, and China. On the way they could stop in India also.

They saw Yamuna's and Padmini's children often, but they miss Narayan's children. Therefore, they decided to make their return trip through Pacific to San Francisco and then New York. Achu bought lot of gifts for his sisters and family.

Late June, Achu and Seema started their trip. First they went to Delhi, from there to Trivandrum. Achu's sisters noticed that he had signs of old age: grey hair, talking calmly, and not showing his aggressive nature. Achu and Seema spent a week with the sisters. They went trips to Alleppy and Kochi; tourism had developed in Kerala a lot, beautiful new resort hotels, nice restaurants, and many more cars in the streets. From Trivandrum they flew to Singapore, about 4.5 hours flight.

Republic of Singapore is a City State with about 6 million people, located at the southern tip of Malay Peninsula. It is a wealthy country and one of the cleanest places on earth. Majority of the people are of Chinese origin, and a large population of people of Indian origin. There are still lot of people with Malayalee origin, but a vast majority of Indians are of Tamil origin. Achu had been there when his first father-in-law was the Indian Ambassador there. Achu and Seema spent two days in the beautiful city and flew to Bangkok, Thailand, a two-hour flight.

Bangkok is the capital of Thailand; head of state is still the King. Most of the people follow Buddhism, so there are many large Buddhist temples, which they visited including Temple of the Emerald Buddha. They also saw the Grand palace with all gold ornate. The current royal house of Chakti came to power in the late 1700s. They also visited the colorful night markets and the floating markets. They went to Phuket and stayed there for two days, it had the beautiful beach, big Buddha statue, Fanta Sea, the theme park with cultural shows and Phuket Simon Cabaret, which is a live floor show. From Bangkok, they flew to Beijing, China, a 4-hour flight.

Beijing, the capital of China, has more than 3000 years of history. Lots of ancient sites, including the grand Forbidden City complex, the imperial palace during the Ming and Qing dynasties, are now the headquarters of the Chinese Communist government.

They had booked a five-star hotel for five days. There were lots of places to see. Their first trip was the Forbidden City complex, the residence of the former emperor of China from 1420 till 1924, walked around the huge complex, a beautiful Chinese architecture, the gate of Divine Might, the northern gate.

Next day they went to see the Great Wall of China, one of the world's wonders. This was built across the northern borders of China to protect and consolidate the territories. Original construction started in 7th century BC, originally built in selective stretches and joined together by Qin Shi Huang during 220-206 BC, the first emperor of China. Later multiple stretches were built by other emperors and the most well-known stretch was built by the Ming Dynasty during 1368 till 1644. The total length of the wall is 13,171 miles and stretches is over the mountains. The wall tour is about 50 miles from Beijing.

Achu and Seema took a taxi. It was a one-day tour, on the way they stopped at a village restaurant to eat the local food, they had cooked live fish. They saw the villages and the agricultural land. They visited the summer palace of the emperor, Temple of Heaven, the palace museum, Jiangshan Park, and Beihai

Park. They ate in several different types of restaurants, small and big, enjoyed the authentic Chinese food which was very different from the Chinese food they ate in America.

From Beijing they went to Tokyo, Japan, a 3-hour flight. Achu one time made a short stop to Tokyo, never could spend much time. Tokyo is a historic city; the residence of the Emperor of Japan is in Tokyo even though he has other palaces. Tokyo has both ancient buildings with Japanese architecture and modern high story buildings. Most of the people follow Buddhism.

Tokyo, the capital of Japan, is one of the biggest Metropolises in the world with about 14 million populations. They stayed in beautiful Tokyo Hilton and spent 6 days there, went around saw many places, Senso-ji Temple, a historic temple, the most widely visited spiritual sites in the world, about 30 million visitors annually.

They rode to the top of Tokyo sky tree, the tallest structure in Japan, 1902 feet. They went to see Meiji Jingu, a Shinto shrine dedicated to the deified spirits of Emperor Meiji and his wife Empress Shoken. They saw the Imperial Palace, Rainbow Bridge and Odaiba, a large artificial island in Tokyo bay built in 1860. They spent time at the beach.

Achu and Seema flew to Sydney, Australia, from Tokyo, a 9-hour flight. Sydney is one of the largest cities in Australia with a population of 5 million and also capital of New South Wales.

There were many places to see, and they stayed 8 days there. They went to see Sydney Opera House, one of the most distinctive and famous buildings, went to Bondi Beach, Sydney Harbor Bridge, Darling Harbor, where they visited Australian National Maritime Museum and Sea life Sydney Aquarium, where they could see a large variety of Australian Aquatic life, about 700 species were displayed. They went for Sydney Whale Watch lunch cruise. They went outside of Sydney at night to see the Blue Mountain, caves which house hundreds of glowworms on the scenic Blue Mountains.

They went a trip along Sydney's expansive coastline through the red sands in aquamarine water and Uluru of barrier reef. They visited the animal park in Sydney on a hill overlooking the city, about 4000 animals and 350 different species including Kangaroos, Koalas, Wombats, and Platypus. One day they took a tour many miles outside of Sydney to see the desert and the red mountains stretching many miles. One day they went to see Opera and relaxed.

From Sydney, they flew directly to San Francisco, a 13-hour flight, Narayan was there to receive them, when they reached Narayan's house Radha and Albert were waiting there to see Grandpa and Grandma.

Lilly greeted them and asked them about their long vacation through travelling in Far East.

Achu and Seema sat down and gave a brief explanation of their visits and gave children the gifts they bought for them. Radha and Albert were hanging on to them. Narayan told them to take a shower, have something to eat, and take rest.

Next four weeks they were staying at Narayan's house, spent lot of time with children, made several trips to San Francisco, and one time to the wine country.

One week before school opening, they left. As usual kids were not happy. They promised to come back or asked them to visit New York during summer or Florida during Christmas New Year holidays.

Early 2007 there were some signs of economic recession, but Federal Reserve board declared that there will be 3% economic growth in 2007, Achu wanted to make sure that his investments were sound. Federal fund rate was 5.25%. It is set by the Federal Reserve, which determines the prime rate, which is the benchmark for credit card, home equity and mortgage rates. By the middle of 2007, home sales were going down.

Federal Reserve reduced the rate to 4.75% and by December 2007 to 4.25%. By December foreclosure of home by banks for defaulting payment of monthly mortgage payments increased and home prices fell 6%. Achu still thought that these were temporary impacts on the economy and did not worry about his large investments in mortgage services in Lehman Brothers and other stocks.

As usual in December they went to Florida for wintertime. Over the years, they had made many friends in West Palm Beach, a high-income society. They used to go out for dinner with many of them, go for dinner cruises and beach walks.

They came back to New York in March 2008. There were signs of slow economic growth already. The 2001-2007 economic expansion halted by the end of 2007, the tax cuts by Bush administration did not create a robust growth as predicted, in fact the performance was weaker than predicted. Nobody noticed in January 2008 the warnings of a slowing economy.

Achu and Seema were planning their next tour in the summer, this year they wanted to visit the Scandinavian countries in Europe and also stop over at Rome and Paris.

Suddenly, one day, Seema got dizzy and fell on the floor. Achu called 911. Ambulance came, picked her, and took her to Columbia Presbyterian Hospital emergency room. They found that her blood pressure and heartbeat were high.

She was kept there for one day for observation, prescribed her blood pressure medicine, and asked to watch her diet and walk for few minutes a day. They also found that her sugar level also was slightly high and prescribed medicine for that also. Seema used to eat lot of sweets. Now she had to stop eating too much sugary stuff and rice.

It was a big shock for Seema. She started a new life with medication, diet, and minor physical exercise. Achu also took a physical examination, his health was generally good, except that diabetes was borderline, could be controlled by diet and exercise.

Both of them were 68 years old now, lifestyle needed to change. They took membership in a health spa so that they could go for daily exercise, cut down on rice, and other food rich in carbohydrate, cut down on sugar and sweet and also started eating a healthy breakfast.

Meanwhile US economy was showing jitters. Achu was watching. Suddenly on September 15, 2008, news came that Lehman Brothers filed for bankruptcy. It was a great shock to Achu. Almost all of his investments were in Lehman Brothers, except few bonds.

CHAPTER 13

It was official. There was a global financial crisis due to failure of global banking system mainly due to excessive risk taken on subprime mortgages and bursting of the US housing bubble. The derivatives of the subprime mortgages bought by the banks were not regulated. Subprime mortgages were issued to borrowers with low credit rating and without income verification, which carried very high risk, but interest rates were much higher than normal mortgages.

When housing market declined and prices came down many of those borrowers went under, means that their house value became much lower than the mortgage they hold on the house. Most of those borrowers defaulted the mortgage payment and banks started foreclosing those houses, ultimately selling, or auctioning with a big loss. Stock market initially plummeted 70 to 80 percent.

Lehman brothers filed for bankruptcy on September 15, 2008 at the climax of subprime mortgage crisis. Achu lost millions of dollars of his investments in Lehman brothers; all he was left with was some investment bonds. Seema also lost about 40 percent of her investments; she did not have much. Achu and Seema were in shock, everything they earned and invested was gone. They did not have multimillion dollars in investments anymore. They would not be able to lead the same luxury life they had been doing past 25 years. Finally, capitalism failed Achu; he had no way out of it except to make sure further losses would not happen. Whatever money left, they moved to fixed accounts immediately.

Narayan called and asked his father whether they needed any help. Achu told him that he had enough money to live except that he had to cut some luxuries. He told him that they plan to go to Florida as usual in December and while they were there, he was going to recalibrate everything. Achu talked to his friends in the financial World, they were all shocked and cursing the subprime mortgage greed that banks invested into making high interest from mortgages only to find out that it turned out to be a disaster. They also told him that there was no immediate way out of this crisis that it was going to become worse, stock market would collapse more, more banks will collapse and it would take several years to come out of the crisis.

In the meantime, Democrats nominated for presidential candidate Barrack Obama, whose father was a Kenyan student in United States and mother was a white lady from Hawaii, a fellow student. The Republican candidate was Senator John McCain, an American war hero, a prisoner of war during the Vietnam War. To everybody's surprise US Senator from the State of Illinois Barrack Obama, a Harvard Law graduate was elected as the first black president of the United States, a great historic moment.

President Obama, the 44th president sworn in on January 20, 2009, had to face the global economic crisis. The US Congress had already passed a $700 billion Troubled Asset Relief Program on October 3, 2008 to purchase the toxic assets from major banks to avoid failure of the banking infrastructure. By the end of 2008, household wealth dropped by about 20%, about $2 trillion loss for financial institutions, loss of about 20 percent of global GDP. The stock market plummeted more than 50 percent and unemployment started creeping up.

Achu and Seema were in Florida when President Obama was sworn in and everybody were looking at the next steps the government was going to take. The American Recovery and Reinvestment Act of 2009, also called a stimulus package, was passed by US Congress in response to the great recession. The total cost of which was estimated at $787 billion provided funds to municipalities, states and federal government for ready-to-go projects, provided extended unemployment, provided tax incentives for individuals and companies, and helped local and state governments to help balance their budgets.

While relaxing in Florida, Achu's thoughts went back to his college days when he was studying economics, finance, socialism, communism, and capitalism. He had lots of faith in capitalism, he became a millionaire only because he invested in capital market, but he found out that his investments were not protected with proper regulations. Now he found out that he could not trust capitalism any more or trust the banks in their greed to make more money.

He always believed that capitalism by itself is not good, but a democratic capitalism will protect individual investments. Achu was born in a feudal society in India ruled by several hundred kings, where the feudal lords or the landowners were the taxpayers and farmworkers stayed poor all the time. Even after Independence and India became the democratic socialist country, feudalism was continuing. He realized that capitalism was born out of European feudalism where most workers were serfs bound to work in the feudal lord's farms and all profits and benefits were taken by those lords. The feudal society had the landowners, who kept all the income and workers, who were totally dependent on those landlords.

Capitalism is an offshoot of the feudal system. It does not make everybody equal. Capitalist seeks to create more wealth and the workers seek to have work and wages. Capitalism says that the innovation and investment make wealth, which is enjoyed by all people. Once industrialization started, the capitalist became owners of factories and industry and workers remained only as the wage earners. This changed when labor unions were created and workers' rights became an issue. Capitalism had to adjust its characteristics from just making profit at any cost to profit sharing with workers. That is when financial areas became more concentrated with greedy investors. Capitalist economies now have two extremes—the economic boom and recession.

Seema noticed that Achu did not talk much and was always thinking. she told him that whatever investment he had was not coming back and they had to find a way to live with much less wealth. Instead of several million dollars, now just couple millions. They are still considered rich, he did not have to help the children, they are well off, and both their houses did not have mortgage. Achu told her that he knew that they had enough money to live the way they lived, but he never expected such a great loss from investments. All his life he made money for both the investment firm and himself; he failed in maintaining that wealth with poor investment and that he never expected Lehman Brothers would to go bankruptsy.

Seema told him that they could live in India with the money they still had like billionaires with servants, drivers, and rich friends, or they could sell one of their houses and either live in Florida or in New York City. Achu said that he hated New York City; only attraction to stay in New York City was the children and grandchildren. Seema told him that the grandchildren will become adults soon and living in Florida is better in terms of weather and cost of living. Next day they called Yamuna, Narayan, and Padmini for their opinion, they were all unanimous in their opinion—to live in Florida and they could visit them occasionally.

In March 2010, they came back to New York City, put the condominium for sale, and started planning to move as soon as it was sold. Padmini asked them to stay with her during summer. Her son Ajit was eight years old. The three-bedroom condominium on 60th street was sold for $2 million. Achu and Seema were very happy.

By 2010, economy began to improve, unemployment started going down slowly, and people's confidence level in investment and stocks started picking up. Yet Achu was still hesitant in investing in stocks. He invested in municipal bonds even though the return was less.

Achu and Seema sold or gave away all of their furniture and gave other collections to Yamuna and Padmini. They moved to Padmini and Rahul's house, and in summertime Narayan also came with the children. Radha was thirteen and Albert was eight years old. Yamuna's children were now fourteen and ten. They had a nice time with children all through the summer.

As usual, they went to the beach, toured and lived in Pocono, mountain resorts in Pennsylvania, walked in central Park, went to Broadway shows, and one evening they arranged a private dinner cruise on the Hudson River.

For Achu and Seema, life was still the same, except they are much less wealthy than before, but still rich people. Capitalism did not abandon them completely.

Narayan, Lilly, and children went back to California promising to visit them in Florida more often. Achu told him to come at least once a year with children or they would go to San Jose.

Time had come for Achu and Seema to depart to Florida permanently. Both Padmini and Yamuna were sad, all those years parents were near them. They told them that West Palm Beach was only 2 1/2-hour flight and they could visit them in Florida or if they needed any help they would come to New York.

Achu finally bid farewell to New York City, his home for last 47 years. He talked to some of his friends in financial business, and they told him that economy is coming back slowly. Achu advised them to be more careful in their investment moves and that he did not trust some of those big banks.

Achu and Seema refurnished and redecorated their condominium in Florida, since it was going to be their permanent home. They invited their neighbors in the condominium building for a small get together to get to know each other more and told them that they would be living there permanently. They became active in the condominiums club. Most of the people in the building were senior citizens, who all had investments in stocks and bonds. Achu told them about his experience in investment banking and offered them free advice. Seema offered to teach them Asian cooking, thus they both became part of the community. They also decided to volunteer in the West Palm Beach community and wanted to be good neighbors and good citizens. Both Achu and Seema were 70 years old.

Even though recession that started in 2008 along with the economic collapse ended in September 2010, unemployment remained high and foreclosures continued. President Obama declared a two-year federal wage freeze. The democratic controlled congress had passed the Affordable Care Act also known as Obamacare in March 2010 with the intention of making affordable health care to more people, expand Medicare to cover all adults with low income and support innovative medical care delivery system to cut costs. Even by 2011, the job market did not improve, and people could not find full-time job. There was a big drop in stock indexes on August 4, 2011.

Achu decided not to watch stock market, keep their money in safe investments and lead a quiet life. He would get into reading most of the time at home and as usual Seema would practice cooking experiments.

Achu and Seema decided to visit their children in New York during the summer of 2012. Two weeks they stayed with Yamuna and children in Queens. Isaac was sixteen years old and in high school, and Simon was 12 years old. They called some of their old neighbors and Achu's old colleagues at work, met with some of them and had conversations about their life in Florida. Some of them promised to visit them.

Yamuna and Robert celebrated Isaac's sweet sixteen party, invited his classmates and both grandparents. Yamuna told them that Simon's bar mitzvah would be celebrated big next year when he would be thirteen. Bar mitzvah is a coming of age Jewish ritual for boys when they become thirteen years old. Reaching the bar mitzvah for boys and bat mitzvah for girls mean they become full-fledged member of Jewish community.

Achu and Seema, after spending time with Yamuna and family, went to Padmini's house in New Jersey. Ajit was ten years old. He was very happy to see the grandparents. Schools were closed, and he started asking them about Florida, Disney World, and cruises. Achu promised Ajit that he would book a cruise for the whole family soon. He called Narayan and told him about the cruise plan and also asked Yamuna, Robert, and children also to come. Padmini asked them to stay till the end of summer to give company to Ajit, during the day Ajit would be playing with the neighborhood children outside or in the park nearby. Yamuna told them not to forget to join the bar mitzvah celebration in 2013.

Coming back to Florida, they were talking about how the grandchildren were getting older, and in few years, they would become high school seniors and would not be interested to hang out with grandparents, for that matter even parent.

Therefore, the cruise they were planning for December 2013 should be enjoyable. Achu booked a western Caribbean and the Bahamas seven-day cruise from Miami, Florida. He informed everybody to be in Florida by December 20, since cruise was going to leave Miami on December 22 and come back on December 29.

Life in Florida had become routine for them, very different from that of New York City, where there are people on the street day and night, police and fire trucks with siren in the street very often and fast-moving activities all the time. West Palm Beach is a very quiet retirement and vacation community, always warm weather not like New York where it is windy and cold from December till March. Even though they were missing their children, grandchildren, and friends, they enjoy life in Florida, very relaxed.

Year 2012 was the reelection of President Obama. Mr. Mitt Romney ran against him from the Republican Party. Obama was easily reelected and sworn in on January 20, 2013. Economy was getting better; unemployment was going down, and people were generally confident.

Achu and Seema came to New York City to attend the bar mitzvah of Simon, big celebration, lot of people. Narayan and children had come from California. Everybody had a good time together. After the party they went to Padmini's house. Narayan and family went back after two days. Achu and Seema came back to Florida after reminding everybody of the cruise in December.

At that time, Achu did not follow the economy or stock market. Economy was in much better shape in 2013, growth of about 3 percent. Even though Iraq war ended in 2011, there were still skirmishes.

As usual Achu spent most of his time reading. In the evenings they went out for a walk, met neighbors, and sometimes had dinner outside. December had come, getting ready to plan for the three families to stay, go to Miami to board the cruise ship, and return. Narayan and family came on December 20, and they were staying with them. Padmini and Yamuna and their families came on December 21, and they were put for one night in a hotel nearby. In the morning of December 22, they took a small luxury bus and went to Miami. They boarded the cruise ship. Achu had booked four family rooms on the upper deck. The ship took off from Miami port, kids were all excited, they went to the top and watched the ship moving, initially felt sea sickness.

Achu looked at the horizon far away and thought about the time when he looked at the horizon sitting at the edge of the backwaters during his childhood, not knowing what the world was and not having any dreams or ambitions. On the second day, the ship docked at Cozumel, a beach resort town on the eastern shore of Mexico. It is a big tourist attraction; many cruise ships dock there at the same time.

Next day they reached Georgetown, Cayman Islands, another tourism hub with nice beaches and historical museums. Then docked at Nassau and Ocean City, Bahamas. Every place they were allowed to get down and spend the daytime there.

Before sunset they had to board the ship. Inside the ship they had formal dinners, buffet food, and swimming pool, nice shows at night and, for adults, casino gambling. They enjoyed together as a family, children playing in the pool and the deck, adults talking and walking around. Seventh day they reached back Miami and from there they went to West Palm Beach.

After a day there everybody retuned because the school for children would open after January 1. Achu and Seema were sad; suddenly they were missing everybody after about 10 days together. Well, that is life, when children and grandchildren grow up, it is their life, grandparents are there to shower love upon them.

For Achu and Seema, they have accepted the life as it was. They often visited the children and grandchildren. In 2014, they went to New York to participate in the celebration of the high school graduation of Isaac. Isaac got admission in Columbia University undergraduate program majoring in economics.

In 2015, they went to San Jose to participate in the high school graduation celebration of Radha, who was going to enter the premedical program. In 2016, Achu and Seema went to Kerala, India, to spend time with Achu's sisters and their families. They told them that they had reached the age of seventy-six and that they would not be in a position to travel long distance anymore. They invited them to visit US and spend time with them in Florida, which they had not seen before.

CHAPTER 14

Achu and Seema were feeling old, and their interest to travel had declined. They told the children to visit them every year if they could. They were happy. There was nothing to worry. Children's careers were good; grandchildren were doing well in school. Everybody was in good health.

In 2016 Donald Trump, who never held any elected position, won the presidency. Democrats nominated former first lady, senator, and Secretary of State Hillary Clinton, a person with tremendous qualifications and ability and was the first woman candidate for president. Even though everybody thought Clinton would get elected, Donald Trump captured more electoral votes.

Donald Trump sworn in as the 45th President of the United States on January 20, 2017. Economy was in much better shape, and unemployment was below 5 percent. There were allegations of Russian interference in the American election. Republicans had majority in both houses of representatives and senate. Economy continued to grow on the same pace, and unemployment also started coming down.

Achu had no interest in stock market and economy. He wanted to lead a peaceful life. Seema also felt the same way.

On the morning of October 5, 2017, while they were having breakfast, Seema complained about chest pain and started sweating, Achu called 911 and she was taken to hospital immediately. She had a massive heart attack and was put on respirators in the hospital.

Achu knew the situation was serious and informed the children. Yamuna came later that day. Hospital told them that she was under observation and that situation did not look good.

The next day Seema died. Achu cried loudly in the hospital. Yamuna was also crying. After allowing them to stay with the body for some time, the hospital told them that the body was going to be moved to the mortuary and that they should make arrangements for her funeral. They went home, called Narayan and Padmini, and told them that they were planning the funeral in two or three days.

Achu and Yamuna talked about Seema for many hours. Achu again told their story, and Yamuna was very sad. They slept for few hours. Next day morning they went to the nearby funeral home, met with the funeral director, made arrangements for a 2-hour wake in one evening and cremation of her body the morning after as per Hindu traditions.

Yamuna's husband, children, Padmini, Rahul, and daughter, Narayan, Lilly and children came. Lots of friends visited the body and next day they had a peaceful ceremony. Achu would not talk much; he was very sad and heartbroken. Narayan advised him to go with him to San Jose and that he would take care of him. He refused and said that he would stay alone and that if he needed any help, he would contact the children.

After a day everybody returned to their destinations, Achu bid farewell to them and asked them to call whenever they could. Children were very sad. They lost their grandmother.

For Narayan and Padmini she was their second mother. They loved her and she loved them. Seema did not have a will. However, she had put Yamuna as the beneficiary of one of her two investments and Achu as the beneficiary of the second half. Both amounts was about $350,000.

Achu now knew that he should have a will if something happened to him. He created $500,000 trust in the name of each of his five grandchildren. In his will he wrote that all three children are the beneficiaries of all the money, except that his condominium would go to Narayan.

Achu was alone sitting in his living room thinking about everything, another chapter in his life ended. Both his wives were his lovers before he married them. He was thinking how he wanted to marry Seema first, and then he was denied that wish, met Radha and fell in love. He had two children with Radha, but she passed away early in her life.

Radha's parents were very helpful in bringing up the children. He met Seema by accident even before Radha's death and Seema had become a widow with a daughter. Even though Radha's death created a big vacuum in his life, it was filled by Seema. Seema loved her daughter and his children the same way and they never felt the loss of their mother once Seema came to their life.

Achu had to marry twice. That did not interrupt his life. He was a successful investment banker, made lot of money, but lost most of it in 2008 economic disaster. His children were good and focused on their studies and now placed in good careers. He achieved everything that he wanted.

He remembered his young life in poverty, his parents and sisters living in a small hut with mud floor. He remembered the time when they were hungry, waiting for his parents to come from work with money to buy groceries to cook dinner for the family and him sitting by the side of the water surrounding the little island looking at the horizon. He ever thought that there was a big world beyond the horizon. There were millions of poor people like his family in India, and elsewhere, there were many rich people all over the world and he knew that life in the World was an effort to survive.

His determination to bring his family out of poverty made him focus on the school. It was not easy to walk four miles one way to the high school with a half-filled stomach, it was not easy to study sitting inside the small hut with two other sisters in front of a kerosene lamp that had barely enough light and it was not easy that there was no spare clothes.

Achu knew that his hard work and determination during his school and college years to reach someplace where he could earn good money helped him and his sisters also followed him. Now all three of them are very well of, even though they were born and bought up in very poor conditions.

Achu wanted to come to America for higher studies and experience the successes of capitalism and he could do that, even though he lost most of his earnings at one point, he was still a rich man. He knew that America is the land of opportunities; capitalism allows one to take risk, compete, sometimes fail, and sometimes succeed. When you fail, try again, and keep working hard. Achu appreciated some of the good things of democratic socialism, where the government should have policies to help the poor, but it often fail to provide opportunities for growth.

Sixty years ago when Achu was studying in Indian Institute of Management in Bangalore, he read the book written by Pundit Jawaharlal Nehru, *Discovery of India*. Nehru wrote the book as a political prisoner in Ahmednagar prison, where British who was ruling India jailed him for protesting against India participating in the second World War on the British side.

The book was written in 1944, the first provincial government was formed in 1946 and India was given Independence on August 15, 1947. Nehru was the one of the architects of India as a Democratic Socialist country. Nehru studied communism, both Marxism and Leninism, and also socialism. He concluded that communism do not give individual freedom and that everything is controlled by the government. He also concluded that western capitalism do not work in India where 50 percent of the people were very poor and before any Industrial development programs were implemented, need to increase food production, and lift people from poverty. That is why he convinced all the Indian National Congress party people who took over the rule of Independent India that the best form of government for India was democratic socialism. Nehru said that life is not a simple parade from what is to what should be. Nehru knew that people even though were poor, their spiritualism was very high. He respected every religion and called the government a secular democratic socialism. Achu was moved by the great knowledge of Nehru on global events. Nehru inspired him.

In May 2018, Achu went to New York to celebrate the high school graduation of Simon. Simon got admission in Harvard University; his aim was to become a lawyer. Achu was happy that his grand-children were very good in school and ambitious. Those would be very successful in a capitalistic society. After the celebration Achu spent time with Padmini. Ajit was celebrating his sweet sixteen. Even though Narayan had asked to join the sweet sixteen of Albert, Achu did not go. He lost interest of long travel. Achu told everybody to come to Florida and spend time with him that he was not going to travel any more. He was seventy-eight years old now. After coming back to Florida Achu started reading books about Hindu religion, which he never deeply studied even though he was born as a Hindu. Coming to predominantly Christian country, he stopped practicing Hindu religion.

Achu had an English version of Bhagavad Gita, which was given by his first wife's father. Bhagavad Gita was believed to have been written around fifth to second century BC. It is an account of the epic conversation between a young warier Arjuna who was hesitant and confused to take arms against his cousins, the God, in the form of Krishna justifying it.

Bhagavad Gita defines Hinduism in its practical side. Arjuna was very emotional and also worried about the battle. Krishan advised him of meditation by which he could master his mind, he was very agitated with lot of thoughts. Krishan asked him to convert his thought and emotions to images on a screen and focus on his mind and consciousness, get rid of a reactive mind.

This was the great teaching of Hinduism. Rather than being preoccupied with all sorts of thoughts, mind has to be cleared without worry and anxiety. Krishna talked about inaction in life, with no goals and achievements or a life of action, with fine achievements and goodness, life with purpose, pride in work and do it even for no reward at all. There should always be an outcome or result in mind, but the success or failure should not define you. Achu was fascinated by the teachings of Krishna, he was thinking that it was true even after 2500 years.

Achu also learned the teachings of Swami Vivekananda, who was an Indian monk, a disciple of 19th century Indian mystic Ramakrishna Paramahamsa. Swami Vivekananda visited America in 1893, attended the Parliament of Religions and spoke there. Vivekananda was an amazing philosopher, who defined Hinduism in a very different way; he called it the journey to find the truth. Once you find the truth yourself, you will realize that nothing is controlled by you. It is spirituality, unselfishness, love, and moral courage that define you.

Vivekananda said that all soul are potentially Devine, the goal is to manifest this divinity by controlling yourself through the qualities that was defined for a good soul or human being. Vivekananda said that the power is within you. You need to believe in yourself, and there is nothing you cannot achieve. He said that what is done is done. Do not look back, move forward with infinite energy, infinite enthusiasm, infinite daring, and infinite patience. Do not be afraid of anything. It is fear that is the greatest of all superstitions.

Achu had learned Christianity and used to attend church in New York. He found similarity in the teachings of Christianity and Hinduism. Jesus said that you only need to follow two commandments, Love Your Neighbor and Love Your God. Jesus always talked about Kingdom of God and one day he was asked where is the Kingdom of God? His answer was, "Kingdom of God is within you." Vivekananda said the power is within you.

Achu was thinking why he didn't learn more about the teachings of Hinduism, Christianity, and Islam before. All religions talk about love, purity of mind, and charity. He decided to set aside some of his money for charity. When Narayan and family visited him in August 2019, he talked to him about it and set up a joint account with him for charity donations.

Achu took time to talk to his son, wife, and children about life, purpose of life, and goals of life. He told them that when he was a student of finance and economics, he was fascinated by capitalism, allowing you to grow by taking risk and competing hard. He told them that he followed the rules of capitalism and became a rich man.

But he told them that becoming rich was not the only goal in life, they need to help others, need to be unselfish, goal oriented, and purposeful. He told them that life was what they make of it; they would face difficulties and mishaps, but be brave and fearless. He told them that at his age, 79 years old, he did not feel very energetic and asked them to call him often and visit him whenever they could. Narayan and family went back to California promising to call him often and visit him whenever they could.

Achu continued to follow a mostly lonely life, reading and sometimes cooking for himself. He went regularly for his evening walk and chat with neighbors.

The year 2019 had passed by; he sometimes talked to his sisters and their family members in India, talked regularly to his children and grandchildren. He sent gifts to children and grandchildren for their birthdays through Amazon. US economy was in good shape, unemployment was 3.5 percent and investors were making more money.

Achu was going to turn 80 years in June 2020. He believed that he had a full life.

Year 2020 started with the news of a global pandemic. Even at the end of 2019, the World Health Organization (WHO) warned of a mysterious disease caused by coronavirus with symptoms of pneumonia that started in Wuhan, China.

On January 11, 2020, China reported the first coronavirus death, and on January 21, the first case was reported in Washington State in US, a man travelled to Wuhan. On Januarys 23, China imposed strict lockdown in Wuhan.

On January 30, WHO declared public health emergency. On February 11, the WHO called the new virus COVID19, coronavirus disease 2019. On January 26, the first suspected case in Oregon was declared. First death in US happened on February 29 in Washington State. Coronavirus was already spreading in Europe.

On March 13, President Trump declared national emergency and on March 15 Center for Disease Control (CDC) warned against large gatherings to avoid spreading of the virus. On March 17, it was declared that coronavirus were present in all 50 states. Ironically on March 18, China declared that there were no new domestic infections or in other words, the first spread of the virus was under control, which probably started in December, 2019. By this time, Italy's death toll had already reached 1000. On March 20, New York City was declared US outbreak epicenter. Children called Achu and asked him to be careful. Florida at that time had much smaller number of cases.

Corona now had spread all over the World. US had more than 80,000 cases and 100 deaths. In highly affected states in Northeastern United States closed schools, asked people to stay home, closed restaurants, restricted entrance to grocery stores, many offices and banks asked employees to work from home, people were asked to wear face masks and keep minimum six-feet distance from each other, social distancing. Coronavirus spread all over United States. Lots of people were out of work. Stock market collapsed and economy started collapsing.

On March 27, US Congress passed a $2 trillion stimulus package to help the employers pay the salaries, provide additional unemployment benefits, and $1200 check sent to lower income Americans. By April 2, global cases reached 1 million. On April 4 New York State declared 12,000 new cases a day. By May 27, US reported 100,000 deaths. Cases in Florida started increasing rapidly. People were not following CDC guidelines of masking and social distancing.

Achu stayed inside most of the time, but he had to go out to personal stuff and groceries and went out in the evening to walk along the beach. Children were calling him every day. Because of travel ban, he could not go to New York.

One day, Achu felt like he had sore throat and fever. He called Padmini, who is a doctor; she told him that it did not sound good and go to the hospital. He called his personal doctor and he also advised him to go to hospital. Achu was admitted to the hospital and was confirmed that he had COVID 19 infection.

Achu informed the children. He had given both Narayan and Padmini's telephone numbers for emergency contacts. They were worried about their dad, not unable to travel and constantly called the hospital for updates.

Achu's condition worsened. He could not breathe and was put on ventilator. He passed away in two days, the day he reached eighty years. The hospital informed the children, they were helpless, and the hospital told them that if they could keep the body only two days and after that it would be disposed of.

Narayan managed to rent a private plane and arrive at West Palm Beach. He moved the body to a funeral home, and next day buried the body with nobody else present. Narayan cried a lot and was heartbroken. He went the condominium, sat there thinking about the life without a father. He had lost his mother very yearly. Achu's children and grandchildren were planning a surprise 80th birthday party for him, instead they lost him. They were all very sad. They could not even see his body, express their love or give him an honorable farewell.

COVID 19 was so cruel, many parents and grandparents died this without giving their children and grandchildren an opportunity to give them a proper farewell. Achu became one of them after displaying such a great love to his wives, children and grandchildren, he just vanished from this earth, 80 years of full life, no farewell from his children and grandchildren except Narayan for the final farewell. Achu experienced poverty and despair, life in a kingdom and a feudal society, socialism and capitalism, love and disappointment, wealth and luxury and pandemic and finally death alone in the hospital bed.

Achu's life ended in great tragedy as a victim of a global pandemic. The capitalism and advanced health care in United States could not help Achu and thousands of people who died of coronavirus. Achu achieved everything he wanted in life. He had good children and grandchildren and had a unique married life having two wives both of whom he loved. Achu experienced extreme poverty in his childhood, but became a millionaire in a capitalistic society.

What does it mean? What is the purpose of life? Could we change the outcome of our life? Could we change the events of life? Or could we predict anything in life? What did the life of Achu teach you? The story of Achu is the story of human pursuit to happiness.

www.ingramcontent.com/pod-product-compliance
Lightning Source LLC
LaVergne TN
LVHW091551060526
838200LV00036B/792